The

Also by Lauran Paine
in Large Print:

All Men Are Strangers
Ambush Canyon
The Running Iron
The War-Wagon
The Long Years
The Border Country
The Dark Trail
The Free-Graze War
Guns in the Desert
The Gunsight Affair
The Outcast
Outlaw Town
Range War
Rogue River Cowboy
The Witness Tree

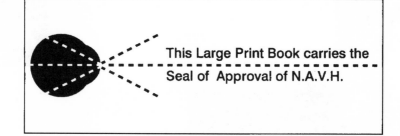

This Large Print Book carries the
Seal of Approval of N.A.V.H.

The Saddlegun Man

Lauran Paine

WHEELER
PUBLISHING

Published in 2004 by arrangement with
Golden West Literary Agency.

Wheeler Large Print Western.

The text of this Large Print edition is unabridged.
Other aspects of the book may vary from the original edition.

Set in 16 pt. Plantin by Minnie B. Raven.

Printed in the United States on permanent paper.

Library of Congress Cataloging-in-Publication Data

Paine, Lauran.
 The saddlegun man / Lauran Paine.
  p. cm.
 ISBN 1-58724-838-7 (lg. print : sc : alk. paper)
 1. United States marshals — Fiction. 2. Large type
books. I. Title.
PS3566.A34S24 2004
 813'.54—dc22   2004057238

The Saddlegun Man

National Association for Visually Handicapped
---------------------- *serving the partially seeing*

As the Founder/CEO of NAVH, the only national health agency solely devoted to those who, although not totally blind, have an eye disease which could lead to serious visual impairment, I am pleased to recognize Thorndike Press* as one of the leading publishers in the large print field.

Founded in 1954 in San Francisco to prepare large print textbooks for partially seeing children, NAVH became the pioneer and standard setting agency in the preparation of large type.

Today, those publishers who meet our standards carry the prestigious "Seal of Approval" indicating high quality large print. We are delighted that Thorndike Press is one of the publishers whose titles meet these standards. We are also pleased to recognize the significant contribution Thorndike Press is making in this important and growing field.

Lorraine H. Marchi, L.H.D.
Founder/CEO
NAVH

* Thorndike Press encompasses the following imprints: Thorndike, Wheeler, Walker and Large Pr int Press.

One

Winchester

The horse was a short-backed, powerfully put together zebra-legged, lined backed buckskin, the kind that stayed in good flesh in country where other horses lost weight and, being short-backed, was hard-riding, but his kind had stamina, called 'bottom', where other horses fell short.

As the man who owned and rode him had figured out about life in general and his iron-tough horse in particular, things generally involved some kind of trade-off; a hard-riding horse for the more worthwhile attributes such as being a 'good-keeper' and being tough as they came.

The man himself, probably unaware that likes attracted likes, fitted the same category to a T. He was stocky, about average height, strong as a bull and almost tireless.

When he appeared in the Winchester country of Wyoming it was early summer with pleasant days and cold nights. The pleasant days would turn hot directly but the nights would remain cold.

After leaving his animal to be cared for at

the livery barn he made a bee-line for the cafe, ate his first meal in a town in a while, then went over to the saloon, not to drink, he was not much of a drinking man, but because saloonmen were invariably sources of information about who was hiring among the cow outfits, and who in town was looking for a hired hand.

The bartender was half-Mex with the fair complexion, black eyes and hair that commonly came from that kind of a cross. His name was Carter Alvarado. He was beginning to run a little to fat but carried it well on a six-foot frame.

He brought the stranger a bottle and glass, went over to his tub of greasy water and went back to work washing glassware.

The stranger got comfortable against the bar and asked if Carter knew who was hiring. Alvarado finished the glass, placed it wrong side up on the backbar, dried both hands on a stained apron and knitted his brows in thought as he said, 'Riding job, or something in town?'

'Riding job. That's my trade.'

Carter strolled closer and leaned on the bartop. 'Two weeks back they were in here every day or two looking for riders.'

'Been anyone in since then?' the stranger asked, and Carter shook his head.

'They fill up fast once summer's close . . . There is one feller; but I'll tell you first, he's a cantankerous old devil. Runs a lot of cattle, enough to hire two men for the season but never hires but one man and works his tail off.'

'Does he pay average?'

'Yeah, so I've heard.'

'Any others?'

'Not that I know of. It's getting a little late.' Carter brightened. 'You know anything about corralyard work? The feller who runs the stage company in town needed a yardman a week or so back.'

The stranger downed his shot and pushed both glass and bottle away. 'How do I find the cranky feller an' what's his name?'

'Mister Irons. Rufus Irons. You go below town and ride southwest. He owns all the land you'll be on once you get clear of the town limits. Keep riding southwest. You'll come onto a set of wagon tracks that'll lead you right into his yard.' Carter almost smiled. 'Only once did I ever hear a rider who worked for Mister Irons say anything good about him, and that was he paid on time, which most stockmen do, so if that's all a man can say in his favour . . .'

The stranger placed a silver coin atop the counter and smiled. 'I'll let you know, if he hires me. Thanks.'

Carter watched the rangerider leave. His impression was of a typical rangeman, faded shirt and britches, run-over boots, worn-shiny shellbelt and holster, a shapeless hat but a good pair of silver inlaid spurs. Carter's guess was that the stranger came from the south, not the north. Up north men wore unpretentious iron spurs. Southward where the Mexican influence prevailed, they wore silver inlaid spurs, rode silver inlaid bits, and commonly had sterling conchos on their saddles.

Carter forgot about the stranger until Jeremy Stone came up from the livery barn and pointed to a bottle on the back bar as he said, 'Why'd you send that cowboy out to the old man's place?'

'Because he needed work and the old man's the only one I know who needs a rider.'

The liveryman filled a tiny glass, downed its contents and settled his belly comfortably against the counter. 'He won't last a month.'

Carter scowled. 'How do you know?'

'Because he's not the kind that'll take the old man's guff.'

'You know him, do you, Jeremy?'

'Nope. Never set eyes on him before this morning. But I know his kind. Works good, knows what's got to be done, does it, and minds his own business. The first time old Rufus hollers at him he'll be back in town looking for another job.'

Carter Alvarado went back to washing glassware, still scowling. Jeremy Stone was good at the livery business. He was also a good horse trader, and in fact he was one of Carter's best customers, but at times he could be as irritating as the seven year itch.

Gil Stevens walked in beating off dust. As the town marshal he was thoroughly capable. He was large, strong, reasonably young, in his early thirties, and as far as anyone knew, he was fearless. Like many men of his size he was good natured. The moment he settled in beside the liveryman he said, 'Jeremy, drinkin' in the morning is the first sign.'

Jeremy bristled. 'Sign of what?'

Alvarado's arrival to take the lawman's order caused an interruption. 'Beer,' the marshal said, and winked. Carter winked back before going after the beer.

Jeremy tugged at the large man's sleeve. 'First sign of what?'

'That you'll be a drunk,' the marshal replied, smiling at the equally tall but very thin liveryman.

Jeremy slammed a coin atop the counter and stamped out of the saloon.

Gil Stevens laughed and Carter smiled as he shook his head, then cleared the air with a question. 'You find sign of them?'

Gil leaned and studied his untouched beer for a moment. 'Not hide nor hair.' The marshal made a wry small smile. 'They sprouted wings.'

Carter leaned on the bar. 'They had to leave tracks, didn't they?'

Stevens half emptied his glass before replying. 'Yup. Right up until they hit the malpais; after that maybe an In'ian could have tracked them; I tried and the only thing I came up with and which I already knew, was that they were riding barefooted horses. Couldn't even find a chip over that damned glassrock.'

Carter re-filled the marshal's glass, pushed it forward and said, 'Mex raiders?'

Gil did not think so. 'For one thing they went northwest. For one thing we're too far north for that. For another thing they left boot tracks in Henley's yard and his wife said they spoke English, no accent.'

'How many?'

'Four.'

Carter Alvarado dried both hands on his apron, something he did often and unconsciously. 'What did they make off with?'

'Six hundred dollars Al Henley had hid under the floor, his wife's gold wedding ring, some other odds and ends.'

Alvarado's eyes were wide. 'Six hundred dollars?'

Gil smiled. He was tired but the beer helped. 'Their hoard from last fall's shipment of cattle. Operating money for next year.' Gil drained his second glass and put his palm over it as he also said, 'They tied Missus Henley to a chair, pulled off her boots and stockings and was fixing to shove her feet in the oven.'

Carter sighed. 'So he told them it was under the floor.'

'Yep. Same as you or I would have done.'

'Now what?'

Gil Stevens shrugged powerful shoulders. 'Wait, I reckon. Wait until they do it again somewhere and maybe get caught.'

'No posse, Gil?'

'Carter, they did it about daybreak yesterday morning. Henley didn't get to town until late in the afternoon. I rode out this morning. Those bastards are a hundred miles away by now and most likely still going. Tracking them wouldn't pay off in time, even if I could have picked up their sign on the far side of the badlands, which is about five miles off, I'd still be too far behind to even get a sighting.'

'So Mister Henley is out six hundred dollars?'

Gil was not happy about any of this. It was his nature to face trouble head-on. He was not an individual who allowed things to slide, but this time he was as he told Carter Alvarado, 'plumb skunked.'

The news of the raid on the Henley ranch, which was about nine miles from town, had spread shortly after the marshal had ridden to the ranch. By the time he returned it was dominating all other general conversation.

13

Gil was at his jailhouse office tanking up on water from the hanging *olla* when Dave Wintering from the general store walked in.

Dave was a tall, cadaverously thin man, older than he looked and having been robbed several times over the years, had an almost pathological fear of outlaws, even ones like those that had raided the Henley ranch, who committed their depredations miles from town.

Marshal Stevens ran a limp sleeve across his mouth, nodded to the storekeeper and went to his desk to sit down.

Wintering remained standing. 'Well?' he said.

'They went into the malpais, Dave.'

'Horseshoes chip that stuff,' the storekeeper said, looking unplacated.

'Not barefoot horses, Dave.'

Wintering scowled. 'And if you're wrong?'

Gil Stevens smiled for the first time in twenty-four hours. 'It'd suit me down to the ground if they tried it.'

Wintering shot up to his feet. 'They're out there, Gil. If they made one successful raid they'd have reason to try another. Mark my word.'

Gil waited until the door closed behind Wintering before letting go with a rattling big sigh. *If* they were still out there, why in hell had they ridden off like men with a distant goal in mind?

He had been a lawman for ten years, five of them right here in the town of Winchester. During those years he had been active; what he hadn't figured out about renegades wasn't worth knowing, and this bunch acted exactly like itinerant raiders did who had made an unexpected killing and were perfectly willing to leave the country.

He was right — and he was wrong.

His town was in the approximate centre of several hundred miles of rolling grassland with mountains to the west, more mountains to the north and east but much farther off, so distant in fact that during summer heat-haze hid the more distant mountains alto-gether.

Northwest the way he assumed those raiders had continued to ride after they left the glassrock, there was a series of stair-stepped low mountains that dwindled down to hills which were the diminishing westerly end of the less distant westward mountains.

Gil's guess was the outlaws were heading for those diminishing foothills and the open country beyond them that went in an almost uninterrupted way half the distance to the Montana line in the high Yellowstone country where one encountered some truly massive upthrusts that marked the beginning of some genuinely wild country.

With decent warning he could have rounded up some possemen and gone after them. But doing anything like that two days late would be like chasing a feather in a wind storm.

A few people in Winchester, like the store-keeper, would be critical of the fact that he didn't give chase, but the majority, particularly the menfolk, would understand.

Gil went up to the cafe, ate like a horse, told the cafeman what he had discovered out yonder, then went to his quarters at the roominghouse to take an all-over bath out back at the wash-house, and dress in clean clothes before making a round of the town as dusk settled. He ended up at Alvarado's saloon, braced for the inevitable flood of questions and theories.

He got through most of it, but when he was becoming noticeably annoyed, Carter's customers slackened off.

It was late, after most of the married townsmen had departed and those who remained were down to grunts of desultory conversation, when the dusty and tired-looking cowboy came through the spindle doors, blinked at the light before heading for the bar, settled in beside the town marshal, nodded to Carter, who recognised the cowboy, and after the drink came and he had downed it, the cowboy turned and tapped Gil Stevens on the arm.

'My name's Jess Evans, Marshal. The saloonman sent me out to see about ridin' for a feller named Rufus Irons — you know him?'

Gil nodded; he not only knew Old Man Irons but just about everyone else in a radius of a hundred miles.

The cowboy nodded to Carter, who refilled his little glass, and as before the cowboy downed his jolt before speaking.

'I rode out there, Marshal. Somebody had beat the hell out of that old man. I spent the afternoon washin' blood off him and gettin' him into his bed. He didn't come around until pretty late, near dusk. I tried to get him to eat but he couldn't, so I left a bottle of popskull on a table beside his bed and figured to come to town and find a doctor.'

Carter and Gil stared at the unassuming, powerfully put-together rangeman. Carter eventually said, 'We don't have a doctor in Winchester. Nearest one's thirty miles east at a place called Hurd's Crossing.'

The cowboy blew out a flammable breath and said, 'Well, the old man needs help bad. I didn't like leavin' him but I'd done all I knew to do.'

Gil Stevens put a coin atop the bar, jerked his head for Jess Evans to follow him, and walked out into the starbright night.

Two

Rufus Irons

Before they left town Jess Evans had a question for Marshal Stevens: 'What do folks do in Winchester when they get hurt or get sick?'

They were riding into a chilly night when Gil replied. 'Take a stage over to Hurd's Crossing.'

The cowboy rode a while in silence then shook his head. 'You must have a fair-sized cemetery,' he drily said, and went to work rolling a smoke.

It wasn't a long ride, just a cold one. The Irons yard was only maybe two miles from town. Evans's buckskin horse hiked along as though he hadn't already made this trip, plus a daylong ride reaching Winchester.

Gil saw the patch of square lamplight a mile ahead. He asked what old Rufus had said. Evans's answer was cryptic. 'He was out of his head, like I said back at the saloon. He didn't make much sense; he said something about four men jumping him when he went down to the barn to pitch feed. That's all.'

Gil looked at the thick-chested, heavy-shouldered shorter man. 'Did you tell him who you were an' what you were doing out here?'

Evans tipped ash before replying. 'Sure, but in his condition I might as well have been talking to a stone wall. He must have some pretty mean enemies. They worked him over even after he was plumb out of it.'

'How do you know that, Mister Evans?'

'Name's Jess, Marshal. Because he'd been hit in the face enough times to have punched him unconscious. The other bruises came from kicks when he was down.'

Gil rode into the yard, tied up down by the barn and let Jess Evans lead the way.

There were old outbuildings, a large log barn, a smokehouse, some sheds, even a bunkhouse which hadn't been used in a while, and the main-house which was not particularly large and had a covered porch completely around it.

There were shaggy cottonwood and maple trees. The cottonwoods had grown naturally, as they commonly did wherever there was water close to the surface, but the old man had planted the maples; a good indication of their age, and his, was the size of the impressive trunks. They were large trees.

The house was mostly dark and smelled of long forgotten meals, coatings of dust, and probably had not been really cleaned in years.

The old man's bedroom with the lighted lamp was a boar's nest of discarded clothing draped from nails, a home-made bed, one store-bought dresser, chair and mirror.

Gil stopped beside the bed. If he had not known Rufus he would not have recognised him. His face was a swollen mass of bruises and torn flesh. One good eye looked steadily up at Gil and the cowboy. Jess noticed something the marshal did not see; the whiskey bottle on the bedside small table had its contents a good inch below its former level.

Gil pulled the chair around, sat and leaned forward. 'What happened?' he asked the battered old man.

The reply was interspersed with long moments of silence, the words were barely distinguishable through swollen, bloody lips.

'There was four of 'em . . . I walked into the barn . . . one feller laughed and jumped at me . . . There was three more but I don't remember much after that.'

Gil settled back in the chair. 'You need a doctor, Rufus. Hurts to breathe, does it?'

'Some. I know — I got some busted ribs. I can feel 'em . . . Doctor? . . . Over at Hurd's Crossing?'

'Yes.'

The old man's one un-swollen eye glowered. 'Hurt more riding . . . that far. Who is this feller with you?'

'Jess Evans. He rode out to see if you

20

needed a hired hand. He's the one that found you and rode to town for help.'

Rufus's baleful eye fixed on the husky rangeman. 'Was you one of them?'

The rangeman's reply was short. 'Would I get you into bed, cleaned up and ride for help if I'd been one of them?'

Rufus did not reply. He returned his attention to the town marshal. Stevens asked if Rufus had money cached somewhere, and when the old man's lips closed tight and his eye showed suspicion, Gil explained about the Henley-ranch incident. Still, the old man refused to say whether he had a cache or not, which was similar to admitting that he did have. Gil arose from the chair. 'Jess here can catch a team and haul you to town, Rufus. From there you can ride the stage over to —'

'Marshal?'

'What?'

'Get down on your knees and look under the bed. There's a sort of drawer up next to the spring. Tell me if it looks like it's been opened.'

Gil got down, removed his hat to poke his head under the bed, remained like that for a long moment, then got back up to his feet, dropped his hat back on and shook his head. 'Don't look to me like it's been opened . . . Rufus, is that your cache?'

'Yes. And now I got to change it. I don't

know this Evans feller.'

The 'Evans feller' had a remark to make to the old man. 'If they came to rob you, why would they beat you senseless before they made you tell 'em where the cache was?'

Both Irons and the marshal gazed at Evans, who had a little more to say.

'Seems more likely to me they was fellers who for some reason hated your guts, came here to clean your plough, not to rob you.'

Gil Stevens, who had been fitting pieces of the Irons and Henley raids together, and who had found several similarities, now considered Rufus Irons from the new, and different, perspective. For a fact old Rufus had ridden roughshod over a lot of people. He'd hired, then fired, probably more individual riders than any other cowman around. He sure as hell had his share of enemies, maybe someone else's share too.

Rufus said, 'Hand me the bottle, Marshal,' which Gil did, then took it back when Irons had taken two swallows and placed it on the little table.

When the marshal arose Rufus put his eye upon him. 'I've had broke ribs before. That ride over to . . .'

'You may have more than broken ribs,' Jess Evans interrupted the old man to say. 'They put the boots to you pretty bad.'

Rufus swivelled his eye to the cowboy. 'You lookin' for work? All right, I'll hire you on.

You do what I tell you until I can be up an' around again. After that we'll see. To start with you can fork feed to the corralled horses. After that settle in at the bunkhouse. Marshal, there's a sixshooter in the table drawer. Set it on the table next to the bottle.'

Gil made no move to obey. He said, 'They won't come back. Not this soon anyway.'

'Them,' the old man said through his battered mouth. 'I'm not worryin' about them . . . This feller knows where my cache is.'

Gil looked steadily at the old man through an interval of silence, then got the gun, placed it within the old man's reach on the bedside table and stepped back looking annoyed. 'I'll send a rig out for you. You can stay in town until . . . All right, you can bring the damned cache with you.'

'An' who'll mind the place and do the chores?'

'The man you just hired. Rufus, listen to me —'

'I'm not goin' any place, Marshal. It'll take a spell but I'll make it just fine.'

Rufus was reaching for the bottle when Gil Stevens and the cowboy left the room, went out front into cold darkness where Gil said, 'Damned pig-headed old screwt.' He gazed at Jess. 'You want the job?'

'Not if there was another one around, but he's right about one thing: Who'll do the chores whether he goes to town or stays out here?'

Gil ignored that to say, 'Well, now you've seen him when he's not unconscious or delirious. He's like this all the time. You'll do some riding for him but my guess is that he'll run you ragged takin' and fetching. He's goin' to be a demanding old bastard.'

Jess repeated what he'd said earlier, but in a different way. 'I need a job. As far as I know, and the feller at the saloon, no one else is hiring. Marshal, if I've learned one thing in life it's that a man can put up with just about anything if he's got to.'

Gil led his horse out to tighten the cinch before mounting. It was late, the sky was spangled with pinpricks of bright light, it was cold and except for some horses out back somewhere moving, the night was silent.

Gil swung astride, nodded to Jess Evans and rode back the way he had come, troubled with a thought that since Jess *did* know where Rufus's cache was, and the old man was not able to adequately defend himself, gun at hand or not . . . And for all he knew no one had ever seen Jess Evans before, including himself. Rufus might for a fact have something to worry about.

He had a real unsettling thought just before entering town later. Jess had said if those raiders had wanted the old man's cache, they would have got it before beating

24

him senseless, and that prompted the uncomfortable speculation that maybe Jess Evans was one of those four raiders who had come back to overhaul the old man, and now he knew there was a cache.

He stabled his animal, walked up to the roominghouse where he lived, and bedded down but did not sleep for a long while. Around him Winchester was quiet except for a chorus of dogs that raised hell and propped it up shortly before he finally fell asleep. Darned raccoons, coyotes, other night-raiders were somewhere in town foraging, as usual.

Wyoming nights were chilly even in midsummer. A man could stay warm inside if there was a stove and some firewood. Rufus Irons's bunkhouse had a stove but if there had been any wood in the box beside it in a long time there was no indication of it now as Jess Evans returned from caring for his horse and entered a bunkhouse that could have almost passed for an ice-house. He went out back to find enough kindling to get a fire started, then trooped over to the main-house to look in on the old man before returning to bed down.

Rufus must have heard him. When Jess appeared in the doorway the old man had the sixgun aimed but not cocked. 'What the hell do you want?' he growled at the younger man.

Jess leaned in the doorway. 'Thought you

might want something to eat. Maybe a pitcher of water.'

The gun did not waver. 'I don't need nothing. You come back at daybreak an' I'll tell you what's got to be done tomorrow. I run six hundred cows and as many bulls as I need. Mostly, I think I'm calved out by this time of year, but you never can tell.'

'Six hundred mammy-cows and you do it all yourself?' Jess asked.

'Been doin' it mostly by myself for forty years.'

'Put the damned gun down, Mister Irons.'

Rufus's grip on the weapon tightened, his one good eye glared suspiciously.

Jess leaned and slowly shook his head. 'I don't want your cache, but if I did I could knock that gun out of your hand before you could cock and fire it. Put the damned thing down.'

Rufus obeyed to the extent of lowering his gun-hand to the soiled old blankets. 'Don't try to sneak up on me,' he warned Jess.

The younger man made a tough, small smile. 'The marshal will more'n likely ride out tomorrow. Let him take your cache back an' put it in a safe in town.'

'Never you mind about my cache. Go bed down an' come back over here at first light.'

Jess did not move. He regarded Rufus for a long time before speaking again. 'How old are you, Mister Irons?'

'It's none of your damned business how old I am.'

Jess neither moved nor showed any expression when he repeated the question. 'How old?'

'. . . Eighty-one, if it's any of your —.'

'I'm just startin' into my thirties. Compared to you that's not very long, but I've lived long enough to know what "please" an' "thank you" mean. Good night, Mister Irons.'

The bunkhouse was warm but the kindling had burned down to coals. Jess had a smoke perching on the edge of a wall bunk. There were four bunks, two above and two below.

There was a hanging coal oil lamp but he made no effort to light it, assuming, correctly, that the bowl was empty.

The bunkhouse was made of logs, it was old and drafty. There was one long table and four chairs. There was also an ancient pair of hair pants — angora hair chaps suspended from a nail. They had probably been worn by some rider ten, twelve years earlier.

There was one window with no screen. Jess could not budge it. Tomorrow he'd find a tool and prise the thing open so the bunkhouse could air out. It smelled of ancient horsesweat, man sweat and strong tobacco smoke. As Jess spread his blanket roll on the bunk with rope springs under it, he heard a wood rat in the darkness.

That too would be taken care of. As he lay back in warm, sooty darkness thinking back over the events of this day, he was re-affirmed in his conviction that most of the time when a man rolled out in the morning he would have no idea of what he would have encountered, or done, by evening.

He was not aware of having fallen asleep until the wood rat got bold and awakened Jess. He heard horses too, listened, decided they were walking somewhere near the yard, arose, stepped into his boots, took his sixgun and eased outside where an increasingly bitter cold snapped him wide awake.

By guess he thought it had to be close to dawn. The horses were still walking. He edged down the side of the barn in the direction of the sound, and felt like a fool. Among the somewhat extensive pole corrals out back horses were walking from one end of the corrals to the other end. All the gates had been blocked open.

He went back inside, kicked out of his boots, leathered the gun and crawled back under the blankets.

He was getting as spooky as a schoolgirl. When the wood rat got bold enough to climb atop the table and gnaw, Jess threw a boot at it. The rat made a shrill squeak and fled.

That settled one thing: Who would be the dominant critter in the bunkhouse.

Three

A Loose Horse

While Jess was doing the chores out at the Irons place, that conviction of his that when a man rolled out in the morning he would have no idea what he would have encountered, or done, by evening, was being demonstrated in town.

A rancher named Wilber Travis rode to town leading a barefoot bay horse with the saddle in place and wearing a bridle the horse had evidently broken at the reins by stepping on them, probably while he was running.

He left the animal with the liveryman and went up to the jailhouse to inform Gil Stevens of his find. He said he had been riding with two of his rangemen south of the tapering distant foothills hunting wolves who had lately been making inroads on his calf crop, and had found the horse standing under a tree. That's all he knew, except that there were tracks for a short distance indicating that the horse might have come south from the area of the foothills.

The rancher had not back-tracked the

horse very far. It was his opinion that someone, maybe a pot-hunter, had his horse scairt into breaking free and running; there were cougars and bear in those foothills.

Gil said he'd make a sashay up there. A man without a horse that far from anywhere could be in a fairly bad fix.

They left Winchester together with a pleasant degree of morning warmth on all sides under a glass-clear sky.

Where Wilber Travis turned off heading for home, Gil proceeded northward. Any way a man looked at it, it was a long ride; he made it even longer by sashaying east and west as he rode looking for some way to back-track the loose horse.

By mid-day he was on the trail of a bare-foot horse whose toe-imprints showed that he had dug in with each spring forward, the sign of a running horse.

Two things interested him. One was that no one in their right mind rode a barefoot horse particularly in a country where there was both hard ground and little stones. The second thing was that the horse had been found on Travis's range, which was several miles west of the malpais country and northward.

It didn't have to mean anything, on the other hand it sure as hell could mean something. Those raiders who had worked old Rufus over, probably the same bunch who had raided the Henley place, had been riding barefoot horses and would almost certainly have ridden north toward the tapering-off foothills.

What particularly interested him was the horses being barefoot. Renegades on barefoot horses were as rare as hen's teeth. If there was one thing men whose livelihood depended on horses, and maybe even their lives, did not do, it was to ride un-shod horses.

When he had some trees up ahead, along with boulders as large as a horse where the westerly necklace of mountains dwindled away, he had seen one set of horse tracks pointing dead ahead.

He had been crossing open country for miles. If the man who had lost his horse, and his companions if he had any, were likely to be watching their back trail, they would not only have seen him coming but would also have seen how he sashayed before finding and following a direct trail.

He freed the tie-down thong over his holstered Colt. The tracks led in a bee-line toward a timbered swale that had a creek running crookedly along its bottom. He knew the place; he also knew if anyone had been watching him and had not come forth to ask if he'd seen a loose horse, then whoever he was, he most likely had a good reason for not showing himself.

He was right. He did not see anyone until

he was within gunshot of the swale and rode up its south side where trees speckled him with shade. He halted, tied his horse and scouted ahead on foot, and walked right down the barrel of a wiry, small dark man's cocked sixshooter. The man stepped clear of a huge old bull pine and did not raise his voice when he said, 'That's fine. Right where you are. Drop the gun.'

Gil saw the man in trees-shadow. He was not smiling. Gil dropped his Colt, studied the smaller, spare man and sighed. He'd been caught like a schoolboy.

The lithe, dark man had a little age on him, his hair was jet black but his perpetually tanned hide had its share of wrinkles. Gil guessed him to be in his fifties. Of two things he was certain; he had never seen the man before and there was an excellent chance he might be the last living person Gil ever looked at. There was no mistaking his deadliness.

'Now then,' the sinewy older man said, 'Lie face down and don't do anything that'll get you killed.'

Gil got belly-down before the dark, slight man left his tree and walked carefully forward with his cocked Colt held in a steady fist.

He halted and said, 'Sheriff, eh?'

'Town marshal.'

'All the same. You'll make out just fine. All I want is your horse. Lie still while I truss your arms an' ankles.'

'How did your horse get loose?' Gil asked as the sinewy man leaned to yank Gil's belt loose from its trouser loops.

'Wolves last night, runnin' in a pack. Put your ankles together.'

Gil obeyed as he asked another question. 'Why didn't your friends take you up behind a saddle?'

'They was in a hurry.'

'No need to be. They got a hell of a head-start.'

The smaller man had to holster his weapon and use both hands to cinch the belt tight. With the ankles bound he moved forward. 'Hands together behind your back.'

This time the gunman had to remove his own neckerchief to tie the lawman's wrists. Gil's head, turned to one side, waited and watched. When the man was untying the knot with both hands Gil jack-knifed with both bound legs, swung up into a sitting position and lashed out, hard.

The blow caught the smaller man low, in the soft parts. Gil had tried to aim higher, but it turned out better than he might have expected. The slight man's breath burst past parted lips, he instinctively pushed both hands against his middle.

Gil's second blow, with his adversary grimacing and leaning forward, caught the man squarely on the slant of his jaw.

He crumpled like a wet sack.

Gil scooted close enough to disarm the stranger, then shoved his body clear and leaned to free his ankles.

He was standing up feeding his belt back through its loops when the sprawled, slight man groaned. He methodically shucked loads from the man's gun and dropped it as he stepped over to retrieve his own weapon. When he turned back the injured man was scrabbling in dirt with both hands, conscious but just barely.

Gil went to the edge of the swale, looked in all directions to be sure they were alone, then returned. The small, dark man was holding his middle ignoring the gun less than five feet away.

Gil hunkered down to roll and light a smoke. When a big, powerful man over two hundred pounds hit a smaller man weighing no more than a hundred and forty pounds in the soft parts, it would require time for the smaller man to recover.

Gil studied his adversary. He could have been part Indian or part Mex. Or his colouring could be the result of a lifetime spent out of doors, but one thing was certain: He hadn't been young in a long time. He was one of those spare, juiceless individuals who lived forever, unless they followed some vocation that tended to make men die early on.

Gil punched out his smoke as the other man straightened up showing pain in his face but with clear eyes. They regarded each other for a moment before Gil asked the man his name.

The answer he received did not surprise him. 'Abraham Lincoln.'

'Mister Lincoln, where are your friends?'

'Gone where you'll never find them.'

Gil remained unperturbed. 'I understand why you fellers raided that isolated ranch. What I don't understand is why you beat that old man half to death and didn't rob him.'

Abraham Lincoln coughed, spat aside and asked if Gil had a canteen. He did not have, nor was he very concerned about the shorter man's injured insides.

'One more time, Mister Lincoln: Why did you fellers beat old Rufus without robbing him? That's the last time I'll ask in a nice way. Do you know how far you are from where anyone can hear a gunshot? . . . Why did you half kill that old man?'

'I need water,' the sinewy man said.

Gil sighed, leaned and slapped the other man hard with his open hand. The slight man nearly toppled sideways. When he got himself righted he was looking down the barrel of a sixgun from a distance of no more than six feet. As he stared Gil drew the hammer back, slowly.

'I told you I'd only ask one more time.'

Abraham Lincoln seemed to have stopped breathing. The face of the large man behind the gun was expressionless, his gaze stone-steady and blank.

'*I* didn't have anythin' to do with that.'

'Who did, Mister Lincoln?'

'. . . Feller called Blizzard. That's the only name I ever heard for him.'

'Why did Blizzard go after the old man?'

'He worked for him once. He hated that old man worse'n poison. I'd thought they'd killed him.'

'You didn't kick him or hit him, the other fellers did?'

Abraham Lincoln looked like he was going to be sick. There was a creek at the bottom of the swale. Gil hoisted him to his feet as though he had been weightless and held him all the way down to the water. There, he gave the slight man a shove. He fell flat with his face in the water.

He drank too fast or too much. He vomited and hung like a gut-shot moose, on all fours with his head down swinging slightly from side to side.

Gil studied the area, watched a sly dog-coyote come out of some willows and crouch as he watched the two men.

Abraham Lincoln rolled flat out and groaned. Gil leaned, lifted him to his feet and started back up out of the swale with him. Most of the time he had to half-carry the slight man. When they got back up where they had been, Gil let go and Abraham Lincoln sank to the ground. He was sweating profusely. He did not look up at the larger man when he mumbled, 'I should have shot you.'

'Why didn't you?'

'There was three rangemen somewhere to the east. They'd have heard the shot.'

'Get up. It's a long way back.'

'I can't. You busted somethin' inside me.'

Gil hauled the man up to his feet, helped him back to the place where Gil's horse was dozing, and let him slip down a tree while Gil freed the horse and snugged up the cinch before turning toward his prisoner.

It was getting late in the day, there was heat in the open country. Gil was less worried about Mister Lincoln than he was in arriving back in town long after nightfall.

He mounted, leaned and held out his arm for his prisoner to grasp it to be boosted up behind the cantle. The slight man arose unsteadily, gasped from a cramp but let the marshal haul him up behind the saddle. Before riding back out to open country Gil removed his sixgun from its holster and shoved it down the front of his britches.

Neither of them said anything for a long while, not until Abraham Lincoln complained that the jarring was upsetting his stomach.

Gil asked if he hadn't ever been hit in the middle before. The slight man said he had, but never so hard nor when he was not expecting to be struck. He then repeated what he'd said earlier, and this time he sounded absolutely certain of it.

'I should have shot you.'

Gil had the reins looped while he rolled and lighted a smoke when he answered. 'Don't give up; you may get another chance. Now tell me you didn't have a hand in beating old Rufus.'

'I didn't. Never had the chance. Blizzard jumped the old goat and held him while he got larruped. When he let go the old man fell and moaned. Blizzard put the boots to him. I would have sworn the old man was dead.'

'Tell me where they went.'

'Don't know, Marshal.'

Gil reined to a halt as he said, 'Get down.'

'Why, so I'll have to walk the rest of the way?'

'No. So I can use you for a punching bag, an' this time I'll use both hands.'

'Get the horse moving. They're goin' up to the Assiniboin country in Montana.'

'To a town?'

'Naw, to a ranch.'

'Who owns it?'

'Well . . .'

Gil stopped the horse again.

'Feller by the name of Hauser owns it.'

'He's one of them?'

'Yeah. Frank Hauser. Blizzard an' I rode for him. When he ain't busy at other things he runs a few head.'

'There's you'n Blizzard, Frank Hauser — and who's the fourth feller?'

'Eli McGovern. He hung out at Frank Hauser's place too.'

Gil let dusk come as he angled eastward to the main road. Over there, with no late-day traffic, it was getting cooler. If he'd had to ride all the way to those diminishing foothills he wouldn't have gotten back before midnight, if then.

He had town lights in sight when he asked his prisoner's name again, and this time he stopped the horse while awaiting the answer.

'It's Lincoln. Joseph Lincoln, an' that's the truth.'

Gil set the horse in motion again. His prisoner seemed to have recovered fairly well over the hours of the ride, at least he didn't whine or complain any more. In fact the closer they got to Winchester the less he said at all.

Gil rode around town on the west side and up the livery barn runway from out back. He lent his arm for the smaller man to use in alighting, then swung off and as the livery barn nighthawk came to take his horse, he shoved Joseph Lincoln toward the lighted roadway.

Up at the jailhouse, after locking Joe Lincoln into a cell, Gil leaned on the bars looking in as he said, 'They should have taken you along.'

Lincoln sat on the edge of a wall-bunk and gave his head a slight nod. 'I told 'em we'd find a ranch or a town along the way where I could get another horse.'

Gil tried working on his prisoner's sense of resentment. 'Nice friends you ride with, Mister Lincoln.'

It didn't work. The outlaw looked past the bars, shrugged and eased back out full length on his bunk.

Gil had one more question. 'How long you fellers been raiding isolated ranches?'

'A few years. It beat hell out of robbing stores or stopping stages.'

'Unless you ran into a bunkhouse full of riders.'

'Naw. We'd scout up the places real careful.'

'Never ran into trouble?'

'Nope. Except one time a feller started shooting when he saw us coming. I never could figure that out. We hadn't done no raiding in his territory. Frank turned tail and let off in a fast run out of range. You got anything to eat?'

'Will your guts get along with food?'

'Yeah. I think they will now.'

Gil went to the office, barred the cell-room

door and stepped outside just as the cafeman's light was extinguished.

He went up to the saloon, had a nightcap, side-stepped Carter Alvarado's question concerning his absence from town all day, and went up to the roominghouse. He too was hungry but, like his prisoner and most other men whose lives were quite often spent miles from a cafe or a ranch kitchen, the initial pangs of hunger were a lot less disconcerting than they were in other folks.

He stood a moment at the window looking down through town before kicking out of his boots, tossing his hat aside, draping his shell-belt and gun from a wall peg, and settling in for the night.

It had been a long day in the saddle, but a productive one except for one thing: Although he knew the names of the raiders, and their ultimate destination, even if he could contact the Montana authorities, it would take weeks to get a letter up there and back, by which time the raiders could have struck other isolated ranches, perhaps killed people, and quite possibly, now that summer was on the land, would not even go back to the ranch.

The problem he dwelt upon before falling asleep was a simple one: How to locate and run those renegades down if they raided territory hundreds of miles from his bailiwick, or ever even hear of them if he waited for the Montana authorities to answer his letter?

Again, a man awakened in the morning with no idea what he would have done before he bedded down again. Gil Stevens was going to learn about that unique fact of life.

Four

Questions

Gil was returning from the cafe the following morning when an old, scarred spring wagon entered town from the south. He crossed the road and stood in front of the jailhouse, waiting. He had recognised the wagon and when it got up far enough through town he recognised the driver: Jess Evans.

He guessed the rest of it, and was proven correct when that old rig pulled up out front and Jess nodded as he said, 'I got him in back on some straw and blankets.'

Gil stepped down, leaned on the sideboard and looked down. Rufus's one good eye glared back. The marshal asked if Rufus had ever known a man named Blizzard.

The old man's answer sounded slightly hoarse. 'Knew him? . . . By golly I thought so; I thought that was him grabbed me from behind. You got him?'

'No, just a friend of his. Does the name Joe Lincoln mean anything to you?'

The old man pondered before replying. 'No, it don't. Was he one of them?'

'Yes.'

'How'd you catch him?'

'His horse got spooked an' left him afoot. Wilber Travis found the horse and brought it to town. I back-tracked. His partners left him out there.'

'You want to know about Blizzard? He was fixin' to steal some of my horses. I caught him holing them up in a box canyon, cussed him out real good and fired him.'

Gil rubbed his jaw. 'Did you throw down on him? He's a lot younger'n you are.'

'Of course I threw down on him. Do I look like I come down in the last rain? Are you goin' after him?'

Gil did not reply, he asked where Jess was taking the old man. Evans shrugged. 'Here in town where someone can watch out for him. He won't go over where that doctor is.'

Gil pointed in the direction of the roominghouse. 'Settle him in up there.' He lowered his arm and gazed dispassionately at Rufus again. 'You need a doctor, Mister Irons. I'll see if he'll come over from Hurd's Crossing.'

The old man glared. 'You got any idea what he'll charge to come over here from Hurd's Crossing? Two, three dollars an' that's before he even looks at me.'

Jess was twisting on the seat looking down when he said, 'If you're not careful, where you'll be goin' they don't use money.'

He talked up the team and drove in the direction of the roominghouse.

Gil returned to the cafe, got some breakfast for his prisoner and returned to the jailhouse. Joe Lincoln was in a bad mood. 'I thought you was comin' back last night.'

Gil pushed the tray under the door without answering. As he straightened up he considered the beard-stubbled, weasel-like face in the cell. 'Are they goin' back to the ranch?' he asked, and got a sour look without a reply as Lincoln bent to retrieve the tray.

Gil left him, went up front to compose a letter to the Montana authorities explaining that he had Lincoln and wanted the other three, outlined the reason why, and was signing the letter when the cowman who had found Lincoln's horse walked in chewing a toothpick. Gil pointed to the coffee pot atop the office stove but Wilber Travis ignored it, sank into a chair and said, 'Find the feller who owned that horse?'

Gil explained about his prisoner. Wilber Travis carefully dropped his frayed toothpick into a cuspidor and allowed a moment to pass before speaking again. 'What puzzled me, was the horse bein' barefoot.'

Gil offered his theory about that. 'That bunch raided the Henley place and half killed old Rufus Irons. I think they overhauled Rufus first, then rode north and raided the Henley place. They then headed for the malpais, which is where I lost them.'

Wilber nodded. 'Can't track barefoot horses over glassrock.'

Gil agreed. 'Exactly, an' you know what that looked like to me? Like they not only knew our countryside pretty well, but figured the best way to get clear from trackers.'

Wilber nodded. He had heard about the Henley raid but not about old Rufus. 'Yesterday couple of my riders rode up yonder. They found one set of shod-horse marks. That'd be your sign. They found where someone drank from the creek — two sets of bootprints in the soft ground. That'd be you'n the feller you got locked up?'

'Yeah.'

Wilber was a deliberate, thoughtful individual. He usually took his time, which he did now before he also said. 'We talked about it at the bunkhouse; seemed to my riders'n me fellers ridin' barefoot horses in gravelly-kind of country couldn't go too far before their horses come up tender footed.'

Gil leaned on his desk, waiting for the rest of it.

'Just for the hell of it, me'n the lads rode up toward the foothills in the night.'

'See anything?'

'Yeah. A supper fire about three miles northwesterly.'

Gil scowled. 'North*westerly*?'

'Yep. We scouted it up from a distance, an' left off when one of their horses picked up

46

the scent of our animals and whinnied. There was three of them we could background at the fire. One of my riders wanted to sneak up an' set their horses loose.'

'It wasn't them,' Gil said. 'They were heading north to Montana.'

Wilber Travis regarded the large lawman solemnly. 'It *was* them, Gil. We got down on our knees and could make out the sign plain enough; three barefoot horses. Now then, I'll agree that now'n then everyone's horse casts a shoe, but I never before heard of three horses all losing their shoes at the same time in the same group of riders. Did you?'

Gil did not reply. He leaned back eyeing the barred front wall window. It was difficult to accept the notion that the remaining raiders had not left the country. After what Joe Lincoln had told him . . . Joe Lincoln had lied!

That should not have been a surprise, but it was. Lincoln had been so seemingly candid during their ride back to town, of course he had been coerced; every time Gil had stopped the horse, Joe had started talking.

Gil shook his head. He'd always been a little gullible. Even ten years behind a badge and the knowledge that folks lied, sometimes when the truth would fit better, had not been able to completely do away with his belief from childhood that people did not lie.

He was beginning to feel disgusted with

himself when Wilber arose. 'Got to get the mail and head back,' he said. Over at the door he added a little more. 'If you want help running 'em down . . .'

It was turn-out and marking time for stockmen. 'You got enough to do,' the marshal said, 'but thanks anyway.'

After the cowman's departure Gil went down to his cell room where Joe Lincoln was lying flat out on his bench. He had cleaned the plates on his tray and had shoved them back out into the corridor. Gil shoved the tray aside before unlocking the door, entering, and locking it after himself. Joe Lincoln came up off the bunk slowly. This was not the first time he had seen that look on a man's face, but this time Joe Lincoln, who was fast and accurate with an equalising sixgun, did not have a gun.

Gil started forward and Joe Lincoln gave ground as he spoke. 'Now wait a damned minute.'

'You lying bastard,' the marshal said, and continued to stalk the smaller, slighter man.

Joe's weathered-dark face paled. 'What are you talkin' about?'

'They didn't keep goin' north, did they?'

'Sure they did. We —'

Gil stopped in the middle of the cell. 'West from where I caught you the mountains get big an' thick. Where I got you they taper down, easy country to ride through. Westerly, there aren't even many game trails through to the far side. No one heading north would give up the easy way to go west where even if they went through the mountains it would be one hell of a hard ride, and it would be in the wrong direction from the trail up to Montana.'

Joe sputtered. 'Well, maybe after they left me they changed plans.'

Gil hooked both thumbs in his shellbelt and regarded the smaller man without blinking. Joe Lincoln was sweating bullets. 'Hell, Marshal, they don't know this country.'

'Sure they do. Blizzard knew it. Anyway, you don't have to know a country to understand that if you want to get around mountains you take the lowest part of them, which are visible any time you're in rugged country. Joe, you're a damned liar, an' I never could stomach liars.'

Lincoln, whose back was only inches from the rear wall of the cell was about to speak when someone entering the office from the roadway distracted Marshal Stevens, who let himself out of the cell, re-locked the door and went up front.

Joe Lincoln went to the bunk and sank down upon the edge of it, convinced that whoever had entered up front had saved him from a shallacking. He unconsciously felt his stomach as he sat there.

The marshal's visitor was Jess Evans. He

sat down, shoved his legs out, gazed at the large lawman and wagged his head. 'I know why that old screwt never got married.'

Gil went to his desk to sit down as he said, 'He was married; from what I've heard he was married a long time before his wife died.'

Jess fished out the makings and went to work making a smoke. Before lighting up he also said, 'The lady who runs the rooming-house said she'd look after him.' Jess fired up and trickled smoke. 'I warned her he was a disagreeable cuss. She said she knew him, everyone around town knew him. She said her late husband wasn't much better and she could handle Mister Irons.'

Gil nodded. He knew the burly, greying woman who owned the roominghouse. He'd had a room up there for several years. He asked the cowboy what his plans were and got a short answer. 'Look after the place until the old devil gets back. By the way, I brought his cache to town with us. You got a safe?'

Gil did not, but they had a big, very impressive steel safe over at the general store. Jess nodded about that and continued to sit there smoking. After a while he spoke again, 'That feller called Blizzard you spoke to him about — he told me quite a bit about him while I was gettin' the old cuss settled in. Meaner'n a rabid skunk, according to the old man. Maybe that's why they couldn't get along. Two of a kind. Blizzard came from a family of starved-out homesteaders who gave up years back. Their place was somewhere west of here where a creek run through a cottonwood canyon. The old man knew their name but couldn't recall it.' Jess arose, killed his smoke and went as far as the roadway door before speaking again. 'He really needs a doctor. He's a tough old devil, but he's hurt. He swears he isn't, but he is. Got to get back, Marshal. If you get that doctor from over yonder —'

'I'll get him,' Gil stated and nodded as Jess Evans opened the roadway door.

Gil leaned back with both hands clasped behind his head. Homesteaders who had lived west of town near the mountains; that was the way the raiders had gone. He did not recollect any homesteaders against the westerly mountains but he had seen several shacks over there where people had once lived, from the looks of them, long before he had come into the country.

At mid-day he went over to the cafe, ate, then went up to the saloon. Carter Alvarado had two customers, bearded, hard-looking freighters in checkered shirts and suspenders.

Carter brought a glass of beer and got comfortable on his side of the bar. 'Saw that cowboy I sent out to hire on with Rufus Irons in town with a wagon.'

Gil explained about the old man and Carter smiled. 'At least the cowboy won't have to listen to Rufus out there, for a while anyway. How bad's he hurt?'

'He looks like hell. I'm goin' to send for the doctor from over at Hurd's Crossing. Carter, you've been around here a long time . . .'

'Longer'n I like to think about.'

'Did you know any homesteaders west of town against the mountains whose shack was in a place where there was cottonwood trees?'

Carter looked out the front window in concentration. 'Twelve, fourteen years ago; tall skinny feller with a mousy wife, tried to raise corn and spuds an' had a couple of milk cows?'

Gil did not answer except to say. 'Did they have children?'

'Yeah. One, a dark-eyed gangling son who was trouble four ways from the middle.'

'What was their name?'

Carter's memory was functioning perfectly now. 'The feller's name was Jacob. I don't recollect the woman's name, but their kid was called Jamie. Dave Wintering used to have a hell of a time with that kid; he'd steal anything that wasn't nailed down.'

'What was their last name?' the marshal asked.

'Blissel. They come from back east somewhere. Jacob told me one time but I've forgot.' Carter waited until the marshal had emptied his glass then reached for it to go up where the freighters had been to re-fill it. By the time he returned Gil had decided to ride west and find that dilapidated shack in the cottonwood canyon. He had seen it several times but hadn't paid much attention, but he could find it. As Carter returned to set up the re-filled glass he said, 'Something came back to me. One time Wilber Travis found the hide off one of his steers out there where coyotes or wolves had dug it up and dragged it around chewing on it. That was a long time ago. I got no idea whatever happened about that, but Wilber would remember.'

Gil downed half the beer, paid up and walked out into bright sunlight. Over in front of the harness works the saddle maker and Al Henley were in conversation under the boardwalk's warped overhang.

Gil went over there. The saddler gave Henley a light pat on the arm and was retreating into his shop as he said, 'Come back Saturday, I'll have the harness mended by then.'

Henley nodded, saw the town marshal and shot him a question before Gil could speak. 'You found one of those sons of bitches, I hear?'

'Yeah, got him locked up. His horse got

loose and the others left him out there.'

Henley smiled a little. 'He hadn't ought to like them for that, had he?'

Gil did not reply, he shook his head as he asked a question. 'When they raided you, did you get a look at any of them?'

Henley's answer was a disappointment. 'No. It was dark an' they was real careful about that. Caught me from behind, like I hear they done with Rufus Irons. I guess maybe I was lucky; they threatened a lot but didn't do anything, but we sure thought they was going to, shoving my wife's feet in the oven an' all.'

'Did you wonder why they didn't let you see them?' the marshal asked.

'No more'n to expect they wouldn't want me to be able to identify them.'

Gil sighed. He hadn't been very hopeful before he crossed the road.

Henley asked if the one locked in the jailhouse had said anything about his six hundred dollars, and Gil said he hadn't, without also mentioning that he had not asked about the six hundred dollars.

He had one more question. 'When they were talking, did any of their voices sound familiar?'

Henley faintly frowned. 'Are you sayin' they weren't outlaws passing through, that maybe they were local men?'

'No. I just wondered if you'd heard any of

their voices before. I'm grabbin' at straws, Al.'

Henley's faint frown lingered. He thought a moment before shaking his head. 'If I ever heard 'em before I sure don't remember it.'

Gil asked his final question. 'You run cattle as far as the westerly mountains?'

'Not quite that far. The range over there belongs to Wilber Travis. Now'n then I get strays to turn back from over there but not very often.'

'There's an old tumble-down homesteader's shack in one of those canyons. I've seen it a few times during hunting season.'

Henley nodded about that . . . 'Yeah. Before you came into the country there was a family tried to make it with corn and potatoes and a couple of milk cows. They lasted about three, four years.'

'What was their name?'

'Bristol, or something like that. I don't recall. I never had much truck with 'em but Wilber did. One time he told me he was pretty sure they'd butchered one of his steers. I guess he couldn't prove it so he let the matter drop an' the next year they loaded a wagon and left the country.'

Gil said he had to go feed his prisoner and crossed toward the cafe with Al Henley staring after him, still wearing the slight frown.

Joe Lincoln complained that every meal he

got was the same, fried spuds, meat as tough as a bootsole, and coffee that would float a horseshoe. Gil let him rant, and leaned outside the cell watching him eat.

When Lincoln had the tin cup half way to his mouth the marshal said, 'You ever hear the name Blissel?'

The cup stopped mid-way, very briefly, then went on up where Lincoln half drained it before setting it aside as he gazed out at Marshal Stevens. 'Nope. Never did. Why?'

Gil eyed the other man over a quiet moment before taking a key from his pocket, unlocking the door and relocking it from the inside.

As before, Joe Lincoln got off the edge of the bunk and sidled toward the rear of the cell.

Gil stood wide-legged studying the outlaw. 'Joe, lying comes as natural to you as breathing does to other folks. I'm going to ask you one more time: Did you ever hear the name Blissel?'

Lincoln's tongue made a darting circuit of his lips. 'If I ever did I sure don't recollect it.'

'Blizzard,' the marshal said quietly.

Joe was adamant. 'I told you before, I never heard any other name for him but Blizzard.'

'But you knew he came from this part of the country.'

'I didn't tell you that.'

Gil sighed and walked closer to the dark-skinned man. 'You told me they rode due north for Montana.'

'That's what they did.'

'No it isn't, Joe. They rode west to the old Blissel homestead. They been tracked almost that far. Joe . . . Why?'

'I don't know what you're —'

The blow was a blur, the sound of an open palm against flesh was loud. Lincoln's head snapped back, struck the wall and snapped forward. Gil caught the smaller man by the shirt front and almost lifted him off his feet.

'This is the last time, Joe, before I beat you bloody. Why?'

'We hid horseshoes over there. To re-shoe the horses before we struck out north.'

Five

The Trail

On the ride from town while crossing a vast expanse of slightly rolling grassland, the marshal saw a horseman watching him from some spindly trees northward.

He kept on riding. His direction was toward a low foothill which would allow him to see below. He knew about where the homestead was, but not exactly, and had no desire to go sashaying until evening trying to find the Blissel place.

He was atop a low ridge when he saw the horseman following him. He moved into the cover, swung off and waited. When the rider was close enough to start up the gentle slope, Gil recognised him: Wilber Travis.

Where they met a huge old burned-out fir tree stood slightly apart from the other, nearby, trees.

Wilber swung off looking relieved. 'You worried me, Marshal. I couldn't tell from the distance it was you.'

Gil smiled. 'You knew some homesteaders who took up land out here named Blissel?'

The cowman turned with an upraised arm.

'See that big solitary pine down there north of us? Well, they lived in the swale behind and below that tree.'

Gil asked if Wilber knew them. The rancher replied in a dry tone of voice. 'As well as I wanted to do.'

'They stole beef from you?'

'Well, nothin' I could prove, but I missed a few animals and once I found the branded hide off one of my critters that had been buried. Not very far from their gully.'

'Have you seen anyone near their place lately?'

Wilber frowned a little. 'No. Not lately. In fact it's been quite awhile since I've been anywhere near their gully.'

Gil went back for his horse, mounted it and returned. 'Let's look around down there,' he said, and led the way.

The cowman was silent until they were beside the lone pine tree looking down into the wide, grassy swale with its dilapidated buildings. He drew a breath, wrinkled his nose and said, 'Horses.'

The scent was strong as they rode down into the swale toward the old buildings. Wilber Travis spoke almost to himself when he said, 'Hell, none of my horses been over here in a long time.'

Gil dismounted in front of the house with its window holes and sagging roof. He left his horse tied and walked back and forth until he found what he was looking for, bare-foot horse imprints. He followed them to one of the tumble-down outbuildings and halted as Wilber Travis came up and also halted.

Inside the three-sided shed the smell was stronger and the imprints were more clear. Gil studied the interior without entering and sighed. This time Joe Lincoln had not lied. Men had shod horses in the shed, there was abundant sign of it. Wilber was intrigued. 'I been over on this part of the range several times lately an' never saw hide nor hair of anyone.'

Gil accepted that; to see down into the swale a man would have to ride to the lip of land above it. If he had no reason to do that . . . 'My prisoner told me his friends cached shoes over here and figured to do some blacksmithing after they left no tracks across the malpais.'

Gil stood a while with his companion studying the sign. Whoever had been here had made their visit at least two days earlier.

Wilber was a shrewd individual. He said, 'Them four who raided Al Henley and beat old Rufus?'

'Yeah. Let's go see where their shod-marks went.'

As they were doing this, tracing out the sign up the west side of the swale, then along the topout for several hundred yards before the tracks led due east, Wilber said it looked to him as though the raiders were not leaving the area.

Gil related what Joe Lincoln had said about them heading north to Montana where one of them, a man named Frank Hauser, had a ranch. Wilber did not interrupt but he was shaking his head before Gil finished. 'Montana's north, Marshal. These three gents are never goin' to reach Montana the way they're riding.' Wilber was silent for a while, squinting ahead. 'There's three ranches some distance ahead. One of 'em belongs to absentee investors in Chicago. They got a tough rangeboss runnin' things, and five riders.' Wilber gave his head a rueful little wag. 'If they try raidin' that place they'll get buried.'

'How about the other places?' Gil asked.

'You know Bert Fincher?'

'Yeah. Who else?'

'German immigrant named Heinz Shultz. He's a fair distance west.'

'Got enough cattle to have hired hands?'

'Nope. Neither of them have. They run one-man outfits like old Rufus. Marshal, what's got me stumped is how these fellers know where the one-man outfits are.'

'That kid the Blissels had is one of them. They call him Blizzard. My guess is that he knows this country as well as anyone.'

Wilber mopped off sweat, re-set his hat and rode in pensive silence until they were approaching the north-south stage and freight road. Town was about three miles south-ward.

Wilber drew rein as he said he couldn't go much farther, he had work to do at his home place. He also said, 'It's pretty much open country, Marshal. If they're raidin' they'll sure be watching. I wish I could go on with you; tell you what I can do, I can ride down to town and tell folks where you are an' what you want to do, an' get some of them to saddle up and meet you west somewhere.'

Gil pondered. He was already a day behind the outlaws; maybe they'd have made their raids and be gone. Whether he found them or not, there was an excellent chance who-ever they had attacked could use some help. He nodded and left Wilber in the middle of the stage road. Wilber set his mount into an easy lope and covered the three miles in very good time.

Gil was riding slower. He had no sighting of buildings until the sun was slanting well away. He knew Bert Fincher but had never had occasion to visit his ranch. As he approached the yard with its log buildings and sturdy working corrals, it seemed awfully quiet. Most ranchers had at least one dog, some of them had a band of them. He had no idea whether Fincher owned a dog or not, until he was entering the yard and some silly chickens ran squawking in all directions.

They had been picking grit near the

sprawled body of a large, dark, dead dog.

Gil rode past the dog to the tie-rack in front of the house and swung to the ground. There was no point in trying to be surreptitious, if there was anyone here they would probably have seen him long before he reached the yard.

He stamped across the porch and rattled the door with a big fist. Echoes travelled through the house. He knocked again, then gripped the latch and pushed inward.

There were two people staring wildly at him. They had been tied and gagged. He knew the man but did not recall ever having seen Fincher's wife before.

As he freed the woman first she got stiffly to her feet and without a word left the parlour. Bert Fincher was beginning to talk even before the gag had been removed. 'Three of them. Came after supper last night. Someone shot our dog an' I went outside with my rifle. Two of them was waiting on the porch an' grabbed me from behind.'

As Gil helped the rancher to a chair he said, 'Always behind you or in the dark, eh?'

Fincher, who was a fairly young man, strong and supple, nodded. 'That's exactly how they went about it.'

'Hear 'em mention any names?'

Fincher shook his head. 'We had two hundred and fifty dollars cached away.'

Gil stood back looking around the room,

which was furnished with home-made chairs and tables. 'And,' he said, without looking at the man who was rubbing his wrists as he sat in the chair, 'They was going to shove your wife's feet into the oven to make you tell 'em where the money was.'

Bert Fincher's brow slowly gathered into a frown. 'You ran into them before, Marshal?'

'Yeah. Anything at all you can tell me about them?'

'They ate everything in sight an' took food with them when they left. They didn't say much, an' what was said was done so by a feller with a gravelly, mean-sounding voice.'

The woman returned. She had regained her composure and asked if the marshal would like a cup of coffee, when he nodded she started for the kitchen. He waited until she was in the doorway then asked if she'd happened to catch a glimpse of any of the raiders.

Her reply even surprised her husband. 'Yes. One of them was strongly built and had dark skin, dark eyes and hair. He leaned down as he was tying me and said it was too bad they were in a hurry, and smiled.'

Gil filed that away, although it really was not very much; he had no way of putting a name to the dark-skinned man.

He drank coffee, listened to the indignation of the people, sympathised with their loss, and left the yard with dusk passing and full night coming.

He stopped every few hundred yards, got down and knelt to be sure he was on the right trail. In daylight it would have been easier; freshly shod horses made perfect tracks.

He knew where the German that Wilber had mentioned ranched. He was slightly less than average height but was as thick and powerful as an oak stump. He was an older man whose wife was very quiet and braided her hair in some kind of circle around her head. Gil knew them to nod to in town but had never visited their ranch although he knew about where it would be, a few miles on east of the Fincher place.

Once, he thought he heard riders southward but when he stopped to listen, there was no noise but the sounding of foraging coyotes on a nightly run.

It was a pleasant night, too early yet to be cold. There were enough stars in a cloudless sky to brighten the earth but until the moon arrived he still had to dismount to make sure he was still on the right trail. After that he could make out the shod-horse tracks from the saddle.

He eventually saw the light long before he was close enough to make out the buildings. It had to be the Shultz place; there were no other ranches this close to the Fincher ranch. Gil did not know it, but the two properties shared a common boundary line on the west side.

There were other ranches northward, southward, even several miles beyond the Shultz place to the west, but they were not one-man outfits, which Gil was convinced by now was all the raiders attacked. He knew, from what his prisoner had said, that they scouted up each ranch very carefully before charging into the yard. As he headed for that solitary square of distant light he speculated about how much time the outlaws used making certain they had a one-man operation in view.

If it was several hours, then Gil might not be as far behind them as he had thought when he first got on their trail.

Again, he thought he heard riders southward, but now when he halted the sound did not fade. Whoever was out there was covering ground in the best way to do it on a horse, by alternately walking and loping.

It sounded like three or four riders. His initial thought was that it could be the outlaws. He changed course slightly, riding southward at a walk; horses made almost no noise when they were walking. Gil did not want to be surprised, nor was he.

As the invisible night riders dropped to a walk one of them said, 'Carter; if we'd rode in a straight line by now we would have found that Fincher place.'

Gil stopped as the complaining man got back a growly answer. 'Yas, an' if we was bats an' could see in the dark we wouldn't

66

have to ride all over hell to find him.'

Gil rested both hands atop the saddlehorn and spoke without raising his voice very much. 'Good evening, gents.'

All sound stopped abruptly in the southward night. One man eventually said, 'Who's out there?'

Gil eased ahead at a walk. 'Gil Stevens.'

They were sitting in a tight bunch facing in his direction. Carter Alvarado recognised him first, and swore. Another rider drawled that he'd thought the voice was familiar. He was Jess Evans who, by rights, shouldn't have been in town when Wilber Travis got there, he should have been out at Rufus's place minding things.

The third rider was Al Henley, one of the first victims of the foraging renegades.

Gil told them his destination and where he had been, back at the Fincher place. They in turn told him that Wilber had found them at the saloon, otherwise he might not have been very successful, most folks in town were bedding down.

Of the three townsmen only Alvarado knew Heinz Shultz and he did not know him well. He had served him occasionally on a Saturday when the man had come to town for supplies. Carter did, however, provide Gil with one scrap of information about Shultz; in the early spring Shultz had mentioned at the saloon he needed a hired man. Carter had passed that along to a greying, grizzled rangeman who had come drifting in, and the old rangeman had subsequently been in the wagon when Shultz had come to town on Saturdays, which made it seem that Shultz had hired him.

As they rode ahead at a walk Gil explained what he thought the outlaws were doing, and that unless they actually did leave the country heading for Montana, or split off in some other direction after raiding Shultz and maybe one or two other isolated ranches, there was a fair chance they could be overtaken.

Jess Evans said nothing. Carter and Gil rode up ahead carrying on a desultory conversation. Al Henley watched for and eventually saw, that square of orange light on ahead and northward.

He pointed it out to the others after which all talk ceased. Of the four of them only Al Henley had ever been over here before, and that, he told them, was several years back when he and one of his neighbours had driven over a seed bull that Heinz Shultz had bought.

They were still a fair distance from the yard when a dog barked furiously, they kept on riding even after the dog suddenly stopped barking, indicating that someone had growled him into silence.

Gil and Carter halted, as did the men behind them. Gil stood in his stirrups. It was difficult even by weak moonlight to see much except the sooty outlines of buildings.

Gil called ahead. 'Mister Shultz, it's Marshal Stevens from town. I have three riders with me.'

There was no answer.

Gil tried again. 'Mister Shultz! We're trailing outlaws that raided the Fincher place and headed this way.'

This time the answer came back in rough, guttural English. 'Ride into the yard where I can see you. One at a time.'

Gil eased ahead. The closer he got the better his visibility became. He could make out each outbuilding as well as the square, massive log main-house where that lamp was still burning. As a rule, very few people burned lights or did not retire a lot earlier than it was when Gil finally entered the yard and halted near the tie-rack in front of the barn.

The bull-built rancher came out of his barn to the front of the building, satisfied himself he recognised Marshal Stevens, then hung a rifle in the crook of one arm and said, 'All right. Tell the others to come.'

Gil turned and called. Carter was annoyed so all he did was raise his rein hand to set the mount in motion with the others to follow along or not as they chose. They followed.

Heinz Shultz stood stoically watching each

69

man as he came to the tie-rack to swing down and tie up. He did not say a word until Gil asked if he'd seen any strange or suspicious riders, then the bull-built man replied curtly. 'Follow me. Yes, we saw them. Come along with me.'

As they entered the house each of them had to squint until their eyes became adjusted to the light. In fact, until that happened they did not notice the blanket-covered man flat out on a leather sofa. The woman sitting beside him was using a cool rag to wipe perspiration off his face and scarcely more than glanced up as her husband brought the men from Winchester into the parlour.

Gil crossed to stand above and behind the woman. The man on the sofa was grey, lined and ordinarily would have had a ruddy complexion. Now, he looked pale with red splotches on his face. His faded, pale eyes went to the marshal's face and remained there. He did not try to speak.

Heinz Shultz leaned aside his rifle and came up beside the lawman. 'His name is Cotton. I don't know which name that is, his first name or his last name.'

Carter Alvarado came up on the off-side of the sofa, looked down, looked over at Gil and nodded his head. This man was the same one Carter had sent out to be hired by Heinz Shultz.

Gil asked what had happened. Heinz looked steadily at the man on the sofa when he said, 'He was in the barn. They came from the northwest keeping the barn between themselves and the house. Cotton heard them and started for the house to warn me. One of them was in the front barn opening when he fired.'

Heinz leaned past his wife to raise the blanket. Cotton's shirt was soaked with blood. The bullet had passed completely through him, back to front.

Carter went over by the door where Jess Evans was leaning. He and the cowboy exchanged a look and Carter very gently shook his head.

Six

The Unexpected

The elderly rangeman had been doing chores; he had been unarmed. Marshal Stevens knelt to ask if Cotton had got a look at the raiders. The injured man, while fully conscious, was weakening by the minute. He feebly shook his head.

Shultz's wife went after coffee for all hands. She laced Cotton's coffee. When she returned to hand the cups around her husband took Cotton's cup, knelt and raised the wounded man slightly. Cotton swallowed slowly. Afterward, for a while his colour improved, his eyes were clearer and he spoke aloud to Marshal Stevens.

'They come from the northwest. I thought I heard 'em but we'd turned horses out this afternoon so I figured it was the loose stock. I heard spurs out back where someone came down off his horse. I was standin' there when they came in out of the dark. I run for it. That's all I remember until I come to in here on the sofa bleedin' all over everything. Heinz, I'd admire another sup of that coffee.'

They all watched Shultz do as he had done

before, raise the rangeman slightly and hold the cup to his lips, but this time Cotton did not drink, he was dead.

Shultz's wife fled from the parlour holding an apron to her face. Heinz stood gazing at the dead man for a moment before turning with a jerk of his head to lead the way out onto the porch. Out there, in a voice that crackled, he told Marshal Stevens he would give fifty dollars to anyone who caught and killed any of those three raiders.

Gil nodded about that and asked which way the killers had gone. Heinz raised a thick arm. 'South.'

Gil led the way to the horses and threw a wave to Heinz Shultz who was still on the porch as the little party of pursuers left his yard.

Carter was baffled. 'South? What's south except for some pretty big outfits with lots of riders?'

Jess Evans drily said, 'Winchester,' a remark that brought total silence for almost a full minute. Carter Alvarado swore. 'They'd be crazy.'

Gil did not rule out a raid on the town but it certainly was a departure from the way those renegades had operated up to now.

Jess Evans had another unsettling suggestion to make. 'Seems they like to sneak up on unsuspecting folk. Well, they wouldn't have to spend so much time ridin' if they raided a town, a house at a time, when folks would be asleep.'

Carter, who had been in an argumentative mood for some time, did not argue with the cowboy, but he looked unhappily at Marshal Stevens. 'Track 'em,' he said, and without awaiting the marshal's response, urged his horse ahead, swung to the ground and walked along watching the ground and leading his horse.

Al Henley, who had not said much up to this point, wondered aloud how much money they had taken so far in their local raids. He was the only one of the four riders who had lost money to the outlaws, the others were less concerned with stolen money than they were in catching up to the outlaws, and this seemed more possible now, if they were indeed heading for Winchester, than it had seemed heretofore.

When they were sufficiently down country to make windmills, tin roofs and one or two lights, the night had been cooling out for some time.

Gil halted on the outskirts. Winchester was as quiet as a cemetery. Not even any dogs were raising cain. Carter leaned tiredly in his saddle. He had done more saddlebacking in the last five, six hours, than he'd done the previous two years.

He addressed Marshal Stevens in a quiet voice. '*If* they're here. It's just a guess. Their tracks come close but they could have rode on, maybe stolen fresh horses and gone on.'

Gil nodded even as he dismounted and stood beside his horse when he said, 'Al, you'n Jess go over to the west alley. Carter an' I'll go down the east side alley. Somewhere they had to tie their horses. If you find the horses cut the cinches and one of you come lookin' for Carter'n me. We'll do the same.'

After their animals had been tied, Jess and Al Henley had left, Carter said, 'Damned waste of time, Gil. Even if they came here, that was hours ago.'

Gil had already thought of this. His conclusion was that unless they found at least some trace of the raiders, they might as well abandon the manhunt, because there would be no way to distinguish three sets of shod horse imprints around town where all horses were shod and all left pretty much identical imprints.

Both sides of the main thoroughfare had stores of one kind or another, which meant there were trash barrels as well as scatterings of refuse their full length. On the east side where Gil and Carter went, most of the residences which faced away from the alley had fenced-in yards. Some of the fences were maintained, about an equal number were not.

Behind Alvarado's saloon there were three large wooden barrels. One had been tipped over, either by foraging town dogs or the nocturnal scavengers like raccoons and skunks, who made regular tours of the alley almost every night.

It was so quiet that when a ridgling in one of the liveryman's corrals nipped a horsing mare on the rump and she angrily squealed, the sound carried the full length of town.

Carter walked beside the marshal getting more disgusted by the moment. He would have wagered his profit from the saloon for a month those raiders were not in town, even if they had been earlier, and he was almost correct, not until he and Gil were nearing the lower end of town, down in the vicinity of the blacksmith's shop, was this proven true when Jess Evans appeared from the opposite side of Main Street to report that he and Al Henley had found no trace of the outlaws, no tied horses, no lights in houses where raiders would have struck, and while the three of them were conversing, with Carter looking more I-told-you-so by the moment a muffled sound similar to the very distant sound of a cannon interrupted their discussion. For several seconds none of them made a sound nor moved, then Gil said, 'Son of a bitch,' and jostled Jess Evans aside as he moved swiftly back the way he had come.

Carter and the cowboy followed. Where Gil halted the rank aroma of something like burnt gunpowder seemed to emanate from a building with a loading dock. Carter swore.

'Wintering's damned store!'

He would have rushed toward the alleyway door but Gil threw up an oaken arm to prevent this as he said, 'Scatter,' and set an example by crossing the alley and stepping through a wide break in a dilapidated wooden fence.

The three of them barely reached shelter before the doorway across from them opened with a complaining sound from hinges that hadn't been oiled. Three men rushed forth and without hesitation fled toward a dog trot which led up to the main thoroughfare and disappeared. One was carrying a small flour sack. Each man had a gun in his fist. They escaped before Gil, Henley and the cowboy could jump clear of old fence slats to challenge them.

Gil went toward the dog trot with his companions in his wake. They got all the way up through and emerged on Main Street without catching even a glimpse of the fleeing men.

There was not a sound. The explosion inside the store had been muffled someway, probably with layers of blankets, but regardless of how the muffling had been done, it evidently had not been heard by a lot of soundly sleeping townsfolk because no one came forth the full length of the roadway.

Al Henley appeared over in front of the jailhouse waving his arms and pointing. He did not have to explain his meaning, there was an abrupt rattle of running horses somewhere at the lower end of town.

Without a word Gil and his companions ran northward for their mounts. By the time they were in the saddle it was no longer possible to hear running horses.

They went around town on the east side, broke over into an easy lope and with nothing to see rode southward. Occasionally they halted to pick up sound. The raiders were still riding due south.

There was a hint of real cold in the air. Along the easterly rim of the world there was also a thin sliver of sickly grey which marked the arrival of false dawn. True dawn would follow very shortly.

As long as poor visibility lasted they had to ride by sound alone, and at least in this way they were able to maintain a proper course. Gil hoped for something better when the world brightened before sunrise, but there was nothing to be seen.

Carter shook his head. It was rolling, open country. What few trees were extant were distantly scattered. There was no sign of the fleeing outlaws.

Where they halted to scan the countryside with visibility improving by the minute, Carter spat then drily said, 'We better not go back empty handed. Dave Wintering will be fit to be tied.'

Neither the rancher or the cowboy were concerned; they did not live in town. Their interest was in just where the hell those raiders had gone, because there was no sighting of riders in any direction.

Gil knew this southward territory as well as he knew the back of his hand. Without a word he struck out in the direction of a long-spending swell of land. As he rode he stood in his stirrups. Henley, Alvarado and the cowboy followed.

The new grass, which was not tall, was green enough to bend at the slightest movement through it. Gil rode to the near side of that gradual swell and dismounted, handed his reins to Carter and went ahead twenty yards on foot. He approached the lip of the landswell cautiously, then stood up there looking down.

The tracks were as plain as day. Three horsemen had gone down into that arroyo and had followed its meandering northeasterly course, completely hidden from the sight of anyone up on the open grassland above.

He went back, got astride and without a word rode up the landswell where his companions saw the fresh tracks, and followed him down into the wide arroyo.

The sun arrived; one moment it was not there, the next moment it was. They loped over the new-shoe tracks for better than a mile, or until the arroyo began to rise until it was even with the surrounding range. Then stopped again up above the crooked gully.

Again, there was no sign of riders. Carter threw up his hands and swore. He was tired, hungry and thirsty. His horse was in the same shape. The main difference was that Carter Alvarado, who rarely had occasion to ride anywhere, also had a sore bottom.

One thing was obvious, if the animals of the pursuers were getting a little tucked up and tired, the mounts of the men they were pursuing could be in no better shape.

Gil squinted against sunlight in the distance where a series of buildings stood in a yard etched with the outline of unkempt, tall old cottonwood trees. Alvarado said, 'Isn't that the Hopgood place?' and had no sooner asked that than he also said, 'Damn it; they'll get fresh horses over there.'

Gil nodded. He had thought of that earlier. With a shrug he led off again, this time without haste because not only were their animals ridden down, but the Hopgood ranch, one of the largest in the Winchester country, would be a very dangerous place for anyone to steal horses.

They saw men mounting horses in the yard before they were very close. The riders, five or six of them, left the yard in a flinging rush heading directly for the three men riding tired animals.

Gil drew rein and waited. He knew Bert Hopgood, who was from the same mould as old Rufus Irons, except that he had become much more successful over the decades. He was, so it was rumoured, one of the wealthiest men in the country.

He was also a shriveled, wiry, grey-eyed older man with a slit for a mouth. When he recognised the marshal and the saloonman he drew down to a jarring trot for the last hundred or so yards and halted with both gloved hands atop the saddlehorn, glaring.

'You ain't the three we're after,' Hopgood announced bleakly.

Gil nodded about that. 'I'll guess; they stole three fresh horses from you.'

The older man answered in a snarl. 'Yas, an' when we catch 'em we're goin' to hang each one from a sour apple tree.'

'When did they get the horses, Mister Hopgood?'

'Just afore dawn. The dogs commenced to bark. My foreman went out to see what the commotion was about; it was time to do chores anyway.'

A heavy-jawed man with small, direct eyes took it up because his employer tended to disseminate, something the rangeboss had noticed over the years, and which annoyed him.

'I heard 'em when I got outside. They was already astride heading due north.'

The older man had been studying the townmen and their animals. 'You'll need fresh stock if you're ever goin' to catch them,' he told the marshal.

Gil nodded. 'We'd be obliged, Mister Hopgood.'

As they all turned back toward the yard Gil explained who the raiders were and what they had done, most recently raiding Wintering's store in Winchester.

In the yard, the hard-faced foreman and two men went out back to fetch in three fresh horses while Gil and the old rancher leaned in sunlight talking. Hopgood wanted the marshal to take a couple of his men on the chase. Gill declined. The old man was not pleased but said no more about it as the horses were led up, outfits were transferred and Marshal Stevens told the cowman how grateful they were before mounting.

One of the rangemen, a lanky, pale-eyed individual, asked when they had last eaten. Carter Alvarado replied. 'I can't remember.'

The old cowman turned and nodded to the lanky man who went briskly in the direction of the cookshack. While they were waiting Hopgood told Gil he would pay two hundred dollars each for the carcasses of the men who had stolen his horses.

Jess Evans stared at the old man. Including the offer of Heinz Shultz, the total was now two hundred and fifty dollars a head, which was one hell of a lot of money to a man who had probably never had more than fifty dollars at one time in his life, and whose hired-hand wages had probably never exceeded twelve dollars a month.

When the lanky man returned with three bundles and was handing them around, Hopgood again mentioned having one of his riders accompany the marshal. This time he jutted his chin in the direction of the granite-jawed range boss, whom Gil knew as an uncompromising, stubborn, hard-fisted individual. He thanked the older man, swung up, nodded and led the way out of the yard, riding northward.

Behind him in the yard the old cowman watched with slitted eyes. When his range-boss said he'd take someone named Gus and go anyway, Hopgood shook his head without enthusiasm.

'He'll find them — if anyone can. He's like a hound dog on a trail.'

One of the riders asked if the old man knew the town marshal that well. Hopgood was still squinting after the distant horsemen when he answered. 'Yep. Three, four years back Charley Sloan, who died last year and who run stock behind town to the east — someone stole thirty head of his springing heifers, which was foolish to start with, and that big feller got on the trail, stuck to it like a tick, found the two rustlers in camp, shot one and brought back the other one . . . Well, we've wasted enough time, let's get to work for a damned change.'

Seven

A Long Day

Like wolves, Gil and his companions ate on the run. They had been on the trail long enough now to look beard-stubbled, soiled and rumpled. Jess Evans and Al Henley showed tiredness less than Gil and Carter Alvarado. In their line of work men became accustomed to going without rest for long periods.

The early morning remained chilly for several hours. By the time there was warmth in the new day the tracks of the renegades were bearing northwesterly in the direction of those diminishing foothills that Gil had initially thought they would be heading for.

They were a fair distance up-country when Jess looked back and said, 'We got company.'

They did not stop but instead rode twisted in their saddles. It looked like perhaps as many as eight or ten riders. Carter made a shrewd guess. 'From town. Wintering must have been hit pretty hard for that many to be out searching.'

They loped a mile, aware that sure as hell by now the men they were pursuing knew, finally, they were being chased, but as before, there was no sign of the outlaws, which simply meant to Gil that they had already gotten around on the far side of those diminishing foothills. This time, he told himself, they were heading due north, probably for that hideout-ranch up in Montana which would be a long ride, but knowing they were being pursued would keep them moving.

Gil, who had run down his share of lawbreakers, had never cared much for direct pursuit. For one thing, a pursuer was always behind the pursued. For another thing, when desperate men knew they were being chased, their inevitable recourse, since horses were not machines and would eventually give out, was an ambush.

As they swept around the petering-out westerly slope and emerged into open country with the sun climbing, even Carter Alvarado, who was a saloonman not a manhunter, intuitively worried about being bushwhacked. He leaned toward Jess and spoke above the sound of their loping horses. 'Where are they?'

The cowboy pointed to the clear tracks through wet grass. 'Northwest.'

Carter looked ahead and to his right. Distantly, there were trees, which was the direction of the sign. He muttered to himself that if they had got over yonder into those trees, they could watch and wait, rest their horses and set up an ambush.

Gil hauled down to a steady walk, scratched inside his shirt and mildly said, 'I wish we'd come across a creek. I'm dry enough to spit cotton.'

Alvarado looked at the marshal. He was also thirsty but the closer the tracks led toward that timber, the less conscious he was of being thirsty. 'They'll be in them damned trees, Gil.'

In the same mild voice the lawman agreed. 'They'd be foolish not to be, Carter.'

'We're ridin' straight toward them, for chris'sake.'

Gil did not respond. He was studying the curve of big timber where it circled half around the open grassland. He had never been in this country before, but he had been this far north on stages, and a few miles ahead, eastward, was a hamlet called Beesville, incorrectly assumed to have been named after wild bees, which were everywhere, but in fact had been founded by peripatetic Texans and named for an early-day Texan of note, Bernard Bee.

It was little more than a wide place in the road. It had pear trees, a good creek, and four, five stores. What made it noticeable from a distance was a church steeple. Given the background of the town's founders, it was not surprising that the church had been built and maintained by Southern Baptists.

Next to the church was a way-station for stages, one of those evenly-distanced corrals and buildings whose sole reason for being anywhere was that stagecoaches had to change horses at least once a day, in rugged or mountainous country, sometimes oftener, but the territory around Beesville was rolling to flat grassland, the kind that had been attracting stockmen since long before the Indians had been driven away.

Gil rode slowly in the direction of the timber until he was satisfied his prey had indeed gone over there. Whether they were lying in there waiting to massacre anyone pursuing them, or had ignored that possibility in order to put more miles between themselves and whoever was behind them, only concerned him until he was entirely satisfied the renegades were indeed heading north.

He halted out a ways, sat in silence studying the trees where the tracks ended over pine and fir needles, and waited for something to be said, which was not a very long wait. Carter said he was not going to commit suicide by riding into the forest. No one else spoke at all, but it was a reasonable assumption that Henley and Evans shared that notion.

Gil smiled enigmatically and reined ahead a couple of yards, then changed course completely and led off in a slow lope in the direction of the stage road. Not until they were over and with Gil pointing northward at a walk, did Al Henley, who knew this country as well as the marshal did, mention the village up ahead.

Gil had looped his reins and was building a smoke when he said, 'Yeah. Beesville.' He licked the paper, closed it and popped the quirley into his mouth as he tilted his head to estimate the time of day from the position of the sun. 'Be afternoon directly,' he told the others, and lighted his cigarette, settled forward and waited for a sighting of the village before explaining the rest of it.

'Chasing them most likely isn't going to be very successful. My guess is that if they came down-country from Montana, they know every big ranch between up there an' down here.'

Carter interrupted. 'An' where they can steal fresh horses.'

Gil nodded and flicked ash. 'Yep. But mostly we're always going to be behind them, unless we ride into an ambush, which would be more likely as the chase went on.'

Alvarado flared up. 'Will you get to the damned point!'

Gil nodded. 'We're goin' to leave the Hopgood horses at the Beesville corralyard an' ride stages until we're bound to be well in front of those lads, then we're goin' to get horses and ride west until we find them.'

For the balance of the ride into the village

with its toweringly majestic white-painted church steeple, not another word was said, but as they headed for the corralyard Al Henley said, 'They'll know who we are, Marshal. You especially.'

Gil shrugged. 'Fine. They can send word back to Winchester that we're up here.'

'An' how about drivers of stages goin' north? They'll have the same information.'

Gil was turning in at the corralyard when he replied. 'Can't be helped, Al. If they stay clear of settlements, which I sure as hell would do in their boots, they won't hear anything. It's a chance we got to take, but mainly we got to get ahead of them.'

As they dismounted in the corralyard a sturdy man wearing a checkered flannel shirt and whose britches were darker where a shellbelt was usually worn, came over to meet them.

He stared at Gil Stevens for a moment then made a dry remark. 'If I was you, Marshal, I'd put that badge in my pocket.'

Gil smiled. 'When'll the next northbound reach Beesville?'

'Hour if it's on time, which it never is.'

'My friends an' I'd like passage north. We'd also like to leave our horses here until we come back.'

The expressionless way-station boss nodded. 'It can be arranged.' He looked them over then spoke again. 'The cafe's across the road.

90

It's not like ma's cookin' but it's better'n prairie dog. You want your saddles and all put on the northbound?'

Gil nodded and was turning away when the way-station boss said, 'You're a fair piece from home, Mister Stevens.'

Carter replied to that before Gil had the chance. 'We'll be a lot further before we're finished. These horses been used hard, I'll pay for a decent bait of grain an' hay.'

The stage company's man stood in the centre of his yard watching the four travel-stained, tired looking men from Winchester cross in the direction of the cafe.

When a hostler came up to take the horses he asked the yard boss who the strangers were, and the yard boss, a seasoned, knowledgeable and shrewd individual told a perfectly plausible lie. 'Damned if I know, Henry. Grain an' hay their horses an' put them in the big corral out back.'

The corralyard-boss waited until the horses were being led away before heading for his log hutment of an office, which was also the harness room. He closed the door, headed for a little iron stove with a dented spackle-ware pitcher atop it, filled a cup with coffee as deadly as embalming fluid, and went to his desk to sit down.

He did not know the town marshal of Winchester very well, but he had recognised him even before he dismounted in the yard. One of the others he thought he had seen before but could not place him, which was one of the interesting factors about saloonmen; when men arrived to drink, the person who served them became a dim memory within minutes.

The other two were stockmen. If he'd ever seen them before, and he hadn't, it bothered him less than speculating about their arrival in Beesville with the Winchester lawman.

On a trail as sure as gawd made green grass.

The Beesville cafe was one of those village beaneries kept alive by the arrival of hungry travellers, mostly passengers on the coaches which passed through.

The proprietor was a grey-headed, widow-woman who kept body and soul together by operating the cafe, and keeping chickens from which she sold fresh eggs. She and the corralyard-boss were not quite friends, one of those things which happened often in very small towns. The greying widow-woman, like many of her kind, enjoyed gossip. The yard boss did not.

When four strangers walked into her cafe beating off dust she became instantly alert. There had been no stage since early morning, they were not freighters, and while they could be outlaws of some kind, she did not think so. As they sat at her counter and asked what was available, she reeled off her menu and finished off with nodding toward two freshly baked pies made of wild crab apples.

They ordered, then drank their water glasses empty. She re-filled them and they again drank them empty. She put the pitcher on the counter and went back to her cooking area.

During the course of their meal very little was said. When the cafe owner had to pile their plates the second time she asked if they belonged in the area, something she knew perfectly well was not so, and Jess Evans answered her dryly. 'Not exactly, ma'm, but judgin' from the looks of the womenfolk around a man might be tempted to stay.'

The greying woman left them alone after that. In fact she did not return from her cooking area until they were out front considering the town. It did not have a saloon.

Carter was of the opinion that it probably never would have, and for emphasis, nodded in the direction of the only painted building, the Baptist Church.

They went over to kill time in front of the stage company's small combination office and harness room. Gil speculated about how far the outlaws would be ahead of them, but did this silently in order to avoid more of Carter's garrulousness. But Carter complained anyway, not entirely because his rear was sore and tender, but also because he had not anticipated anything like this, and he had left no one to mind the saloon during his absence. Jess Evans teased him.

'It'll dry folks out. Too much drinkin' raises hell with the liver.'

Carter snorted. 'Where did you hear such nonsense as that?'

'From a pill-roller down in New Messico. He told me he'd embalmed couple dozen fellers who drank themselves into the grave.'

Carter was straightening up on the bench when Al Henley said, 'There it comes,' and jutted his jaw.

The stage was close enough to the lower end of the village for the whip to have hauled down to a slogging walk. Even at that distance the men on the bench could hear chain traces rattling.

The corralyard-boss came to the roadway, pulled out a watch, consulted it, re-pocketed it and spoke to no one in particular. 'It's that damned mud wagon again. I told 'em down in Winchester it's an unnecessary drag on the hitch, what with them broad wheels and tyres.'

He turned, nodded to the seated men and said, 'Won't take long to change horses.'

He disappeared inside the yard as the coach made a wide sashay in order to avoid hitting hubs on the gate posts. The driver, a bearded man with a perpetual squint and leathery face, looked down, saw the men on the bench and almost forgot to hoist a booted foot to the binder handle as the stage wheeled up where the corralyard-boss and a hostler were waiting.

The whip swarmed down the side of his vehicle like a spider going down a wall, threw a nod to the yardman and went out front where he pulled off a pair of smoke-tanned gauntlets, the badge of his trade, as he addressed Carter Alvarado. 'What'n hell you doin' 'way up here? The saloon's locked tighter'n a drum and folks was wonderin' what happened to you.'

Carter jerked a thumb. 'Ask him; he dragooned us.'

Gil smiled, he knew the stage driver. 'Change of scenery, Paul. You know how it is, a man needs a change —'

'Marshal,' the bearded man cut in while folding both gauntlets under and over his shellbelt. 'While you been gone someone dynamited the safe in Wintering's store and made off with a thousand dollars. Wintering went all over town blamin' it on you for not bein' there when it happened.'

Gil nodded about that because he had expected nothing else. But the amount of money that the raiders got surprised him. 'A thousand dollars?'

The driver nodded while groping for his plug of chewing tobacco. 'That's what Wintering said. They blew the door right off his store safe.' The driver cheeked a cud before smiling as he told them the rest of it. 'They took all the blankets off a shelf in the store to muffle the blast. It worked real well, no one seemed to have any idea there'd been a raid until old Wintering run out into the roadway hollerin' his head off.'

The whip threw back his head and laughed. There was more. He was still grinning like a tame ape when he told them.

'Whoever they was, they broke open a box of Wintering's own blasting powder to blow his safe.'

The whip laughed again as the corralyard-boss appeared in the gateway to announce that a fresh hitch had been put on the coach. The same man also nodded to the four seated men. 'Climb aboard, gents.'

The whip stopped laughing. His eyes widened. 'This coach is going north, Marshal.'

As the four passengers arose Gil nodded and walked past into the yard where the stage was waiting. The whip caught up with him. 'North? Winchester's in the opposite direction in case you've forgot.'

They all piled in leaving the whip and the yard boss standing there looking in, until the yard boss nudged the driver. 'Get up there, Paul. You're already an hour behind.'

The whip turned. 'That there is the marshal of Winchester.'

The yard man nodded. 'I know that.'

'Well hell, the store down at Winchester

was robbed down to its last penny. The marshal's needed —'

'Get up on the damned box, Paul,' the corralyard-boss growled and walked away.

The bearded man climbed up, gathered the lines and made a big, wide turn before aiming squarely for the road beyond the gates.

Two people watched the mud wagon turn north, one was the corralyard-boss, the other was the grey-headed woman who ran the cafe.

It was hotter inside the coach than it was outside but after warming-out his fresh hitch the drover hollered them over into a mile-eating slow lope, which stirred a little breeze inside.

Jess Evans began to laugh. The others looked at him, then joined him. The look on the driver's face, his clear bafflement, had been the high point in an otherwise long, tiring day.

The next northward town was twenty miles ahead. It was a place called Appomattox, for obvious reasons, and was about the size of Winchester.

With the exception of the cowboy they had all been up there at one time or another. Carter fell asleep and nearly tumbled off the narrow seat. Al Henley caught him, shoved him back and instead of gratitude got a fierce scowl as the saloonman eased slightly to one side so that most of his weight would be on his hip, not his cheek.

The afternoon was downright hot. The little breeze helped but not a whole lot. By the time they pulled off to water the horses at an old stone trough the driver had done considerable thinking, and as he accepted the help of his passengers watering the horses, he did not ask a single question. He lacked a little of being the smartest man on earth, but he did not have to be that clever to eventually figure out that if the town marshal of Winchester and his companions were going north, they had a damned sound reason for doing it.

He had to be satisfied with this conjecture; none of his four passengers volunteered a word about their purpose or their destination.

Later, with dusk settling and at least two of his passengers sleeping, the whip dug out a pony of malt whiskey and nipped a little. A man whose outlook on life had to be influenced somewhat by the fact that he spent as much as eight, sometimes ten or fifteen hours a day looking at the rear end of horses, required some variety of spiritual boost otherwise he got so darned cranky and disillusioned he ended up taking some other kind of job.

The last watering-stop was about two miles shy of the next town, and this time only the marshal and the cowboy piled out to help with the watering. As before not a word was said.

When the lights of Appomattox appeared ahead, Gil shook Carter and Henley awake. Jess Evans, who had not closed his eyes, asked how far Appomattox was from the Montana line.

Only Carter Alvarado had any idea; he thought it had to be about a hundred miles. The answer silenced Jess Evans, who had never liked riding stages. They made him seasick.

As the whip dropped to a steady walk on the outskirts of town his passengers leaned to look out. There were lights, roadway traffic, stores and a saloon.

There was also a hotel, which everyone but Marshal Stevens eyed with pleasure. They were dog-tired and hungry again, they were also dirty, rumpled, beard stubbled and baggy eyed.

As the coach turned up into the lighted corralyard and stopped, they piled out to stretch. The driver came down among them and said, 'The hotel's back a few doors on the east side of the road,' then walked away pulling off his gauntlets as he strode a straight line in the direction of the saloon.

Eight
Horseback Again

Gil spoke aside to one of the corralyard hostlers before leading off in the direction of the cafe. This time the proprietor was a large, fat individual with a red heart tattooed on one lower arm with the word 'Mother' scrawled across it. He took their orders and walked away. There were three other diners along the counter, two rangemen and one old gaffer who was as ancient as dirt. The old man had faded, shrewd, sunken blue eyes and no teeth. His noisy eating inspired the pair of rangemen to finish eating, pay up and leave.

Jess and Al Henley ate like horses, Carter did pretty well but he was too tired to enjoy the meal. When it was finished he asked Gil if he knew the name of the next town northward. Gil said, 'Anselmo. You never been up there?'

Carter hadn't. 'No need until now. Can we make it by noon tomorrow?'

Gil's reply stopped the eating utensils of his companions in mid air. 'We'll be there by midnight.'

The old gummer saw the expressions and laughed. It was the only sound until Carter said. 'Midnight? You mean tonight?'

'Yep. The only way we'll get ahead of them is to keep moving faster than they're moving, an' that means covering ground while they're sleeping.'

Carter looked at his half-empty plate. He probably should have expected something like this. They *were* in pursuit of outlaws. He got a re-fill for his coffee cup and sipped thoughtfully. When the others had finished and Gil arose to dump silver atop the counter, Carter led the way out into the pleasant night. Out there he said, 'Well, let this be a lesson to you fellers; don't never go manhunting with him, he'll work you half to death.'

Jess Evans scanned the sky and asked if they had time to visit the saloon before the stage left Appomattox. Gil led the way.

Appomattox had two saloons, the one most favoured by rangemen was the one they entered. A giant of a man behind the bar who combed his hair with a part in the middle, nodded and without waiting set up a bottle and four jolt glasses.

Down the bar the stager named Paul was combing his beard with bent fingers when he looked northward and said, 'You lads got fed, did you?'

Carter nodded, the others were drinking.

The driver then also said, 'Maybe I'll meet you on my way back, if you lie over a few days.'

Carter looked down the bar. 'When're you goin' to pull out tonight?'

'Ten, fifteen minutes; as soon as they change the hitch and check the runnin' gear.'

Carter nodded as he reached to re-fill his glass. 'We'll be aboard,' he said. The driver named Paul stared.

Outside, the night was still pleasant, which it would not be by midnight. At this elevation there was no such thing as hot nights, summer or winter.

There were two lanterns hanging on either side of the gateway leading into the stage company's yard. Beyond, where light was required for a standing coach to be looked over before horses were jockeyed onto the tongue, light shone downward from two high poles, each with another hanging lantern.

It was possible from out front of the saloon to see directly into the corralyard across the road. Gil stood alone in the pleasant night watching the mud wagon being gone over. He returned to his place at the bar to say they had time for another drink before the horses would be hitched. His companions solemnly took advantage of those minutes, and Jess Evans, whose face was getting red, asked how far ahead of the outlaws they would be by midnight. Gil could not say exactly but he could conjecture. 'Somewhere they got to bed down. Whether they need rest or not their horses will. Maybe by tomorrow morning we can hire horses and head west to make the interception.'

Carter, an expert on liquor served over bars, complimented the big barman on his whiskey. The big man beamed.

Carter then slowly turned to the nearly as large man beside him and scowled. 'Suppose we ride west an' don't find them?'

Gil's reply was calmly given. 'Then we'll scout around until we do. Carter, you remember that old cowboy bleedin' his life away in that homesteader's parlour — shot from behind?'

Alvarado did not say whether he remembered or not, he re-filled his glass, downed its contents and headed for the roadway. Gil counted out silver and left it atop the bar as his other companions emulated the saloonman.

The driver emerged right behind them, cleared his throat, pulled the grey gauntlets from under his shellbelt and pulled them on slowly as he looked into the yard across the way where horses were being positioned on the pole.

Without a word he led off with four silent men trooping behind him.

The cowboy went around back to make certain their outfits were still in the boot. As he was afterwards climbing in the driver hesitated long enough to slam the door after him and shake his head.

The second leg of their northward journey was made in faster time. Nights were cooler than days this time of year; whips could keep their hitches moving at a faster gait.

Al Henley, who had stopped smoking four years earlier, borrowed the makings from Jess Evans, rolled a smoke, lit it and was seized with a fit of coughing.

The pleasant night became less pleasant as the moon soared. They rolled down the leather flaps to keep out most of the chill but not all of it.

Carter slept, Henley gave up his smoke, Jess Evans asked if Marshal Stevens had sent word over to Hurd's Crossing for the doctor to visit old Rufus at the hotel back in Winchester, and Gil swore under his breath; he had completely forgotten to do that.

The cowboy smiled as he trickled smoke. 'Don't much matter. I met one of the yardmen and told him to ask the driver of the next coach goin' over there to tell the doctor about old Rufus. Tell me something, Marshal, does Mister Irons have kinfolk?'

Gil had no idea. 'I never asked and as far as I can recollect he never mentioned any. As far as I know there was just the old man and his wife. Why? You don't think he'll make it?'

'How old is he, Marshal?'

Gil did not have the answer to that either. 'Old enough.'

'My guess is he's either in his eighties or awful darned close to it. He took one hell of a shallacking, an' except for his ornery disposition, he didn't impress me as bein' very strong.' The cowboy killed his smoke. 'Wouldn't hurt to find out if he has kin, would it?'

Gil nodded. It wouldn't hurt, for a fact, but he knew that cranky old devil as well as most folks did, and he'd bet the price of a good horse he wasn't going to die. Not for a while yet anyway.

It was an hour past midnight when they pulled into the corralyard at the next town northward, another of those little villages whose main business was the stage company. Its name was Anselmo, and it was dark from one end to the other when they stopped inside the corralyard where the only lamps were burning.

Two greying former rangemen shuffled forward from the bunkhouse built against the rear wall to care for the animals. One of them eyed the whip dispassionately as he said, 'Good trip, Paul?'

The whip's reply was short. 'Delightful. Any stew in the pot at the bunkhouse?'

'Enough,' the hostler replied as he leaned to free the traces on one side as his companion was doing on the other side.

Gil waited until the whip was striding toward the rear of the yard before he told the nearest hostler who he was and that he and his companions needed four saddle horses.

The nightman straightened up, looked Gil and his companions over and shook his head. 'We only got three saddle animals and four combination horses, an' the boss ain't here and don't like to be routed out. You better wait until morning, Marshal.'

Gil considered the tired-looking nightman. 'We can't wait until morning, friend. We've come a long way as fast as possible to be able to cut off some outlaws headin' north.'

The hostler showed no expression as he shook his head. 'It ain't up to me, Marshal.'

Carter leaned and tapped the hostler in the middle of the chest. 'Show us where those horses are. If your boss raises hell, tell him we'll settle with him when we bring the horses back.'

Carter was large, mostly running to fat, but with black stubble and an unpleasant look, he was intimidating enough.

The hostler said, 'Follow me.'

There were sixteen horses and four mules in a corral. The hostler pointed out which were the saddle horses and which were the combination animals, then leaned with both arms atop a stringer as he watched Marshal Stevens and the men he assumed were his posse-riders, snake the animals out and head toward the rear of the mud wagon with them.

The hostler waited until they were behind the coach before going briskly to the leanto bunkhouse where Paul was sitting at a scarred table eating from a bowl. Three men in bunks were sleeping like logs around the gloomy room. One snored like each breath would be his last.

The hostler glared at Paul. 'They're takin' our horses, for chris'sake.'

Paul shrugged. 'You got a gun, stop it if you've a mind to, but that big one's the law down at Winchester an' he's got one hell of a reputation. This stew is goin' sour.'

'The boss will raise hell with me.'

'Naw. I'll tell him in the morning before I start back. They're on a trail.'

The hostler's frown did not slacken. 'Out-laws?'

'No, the tooth fairy. Which bunk ain't taken?'

The hostler stormed out into the night and arrived down by the mud wagon in time to see the men from Winchester head out the gateway and turn northward. It was well past midnight, and getting colder by the minute. The second hostler returned from caring for the hitch and chewed tobacco as he stood with the indignant nightman watching the four horsemen. He said, 'Them's our horses, Jack.'

The perturbed hostler gave his companion

a bitter stare. 'Mister Potter'll fire me sure as hell.'

'Why'd you let 'em take them?'

'Because they're possemen after a herd of outlaws.'

The tobacco-chewer turned to expectorate then turned back as he said, 'Naw. Mister Potter'll understand.'

When the riders were no longer visible the pair of nightmen trooped back to their bunks in the leanto. One of them glared at the lump where Paul the whip was dead to the world.

Carter Alvarado rode slightly on one side, alternating between providing relief in this way from one cheek to the other, but whiskey had not only increased his circulation so he was less bothered by the cold, it had also improved his disposition, something the others did not realise until they were miles west of Anselmo with dawn coming, and halted at a creek to tank up the horses, who were not thirsty, and to drink themselves then splash cold water over their faces.

Here, the saloonman produced a pony of whiskey and passed it around. They all had one swallow. Carter grinned, pocketed the bottle and got back astride.

None of them knew the country ahead. Dawnlight made it possible for them to make out timber and open places, called 'parks', the farther north a rider got, among the stands of big old trees.

Once, Gil thought he smelled a cooking fire but the others caught no scent so they continued through the timber.

It was big country, miles and miles of it, largely timbered so that visibility was limited from time to time, but they did see a ranch far northward, with a spiral of white smoke rising above one of the buildings but for a long time that was the only indication that this was settled country.

Gil was looking for a good north-going trail when he thought they would be far enough west to make their interception, but the longer he rode and the higher the sun climbed, the more he began to wonder if there was such a trail, if so where it was, and if not how in hell four men were going to be able to locate three other men in a country riders could pass each other a mile ahead or a mile behind. Henley offered a suggestion. If they split up, a couple of them to ride south-ward on a scout while the other two rode northward to find a ranch where they had horses, the chances would be better that con-tact might be made than if they continued riding together.

Gil paired Henley off with the cowboy to make the sashay southward. He and Carter eased a little northward toward open country.

They didn't find a ranch, they found a cov-ered sheep wagon, more woollies than either of them had ever seen before, and some dogs that began barking even before Carter and Gil had cleared the last fringe of trees.

A young, dark man with too-long curly hair punched beneath a nondescript hat came out of the wagon carrying a rifle. He leaned the gun aside and watched the horsemen approach. When the dogs would have darted in to nip, the man yelled at them. They immediately left off their challenging. Gil was impressed. So was Carter although he was more interested in the sheepherder. They were still a fair distance off when Carter said, 'Mex.'

He was wrong but understandably so. Wyoming would weather range wars between cattlemen and sheepmen until there were more sheep in Wyoming than there were people and cattle combined. But that was in the future, and the shepherds would be Basques, a people no one had heard of at the time Gil and Carter rode up, stopped and called a greeting to the lanky young man with the rifle. He grinned broadly and gestured for them to dismount, which they did. Gil asked if he had seen three riders passing northward. The young man continued to grin. He had fair skin but very dark eyes and dark curly hair.

Carter thought a moment then repeated the question in Mexican Spanish. This time the shepherd's grin faded a little. What

Carter had asked had familiar sounds to it, but was not entirely understandable.

The herder spoke to them and Carter looked bewildered. Gil asked what he had said. Carter answered honestly. 'Damned if I know.' He asked if the herder was Spanish. This time he got a swift reply, but again in a language that was completely foreign to him. He then asked the sheepherder in Mex-Spanish, speaking very slowly, if there had been three horsemen pass through.

The Basque looked worried. His reply came as slowly as Carter had spoken, a mixture of pure Spanish and some other language, but the meaning was clear: He had not seen any riders. Not in a week.

He then repeated one word three times. 'Basque, *Señores*: Basque. Basque.'

They would not have understood if the young man had not repeatedly tapped himself on the chest. Carter smiled, rolled his eyes and turned to mount his horse. Gil fished in a pocket, held forth a silver dollar which the shepherd accepted as he pulled off his old hat and spoke in a tone of unmistakable gratitude.

They went west from the sheep wagon through hundreds of sheep. The herder watched them but his dogs did more, they skulked among the sheep following the horsemen.

Carter finally said, 'What's this country

comin' to? You know what a Basque is?'

Gil shook his head. He did not particularly care for the smell of sheep; it was everywhere, along with little tufts of wool that had been snagged by underbrush. Another mile west he wondered aloud if that Basque back yonder, or whatever he was, knew this country had packs of wolves in it.

They spent the balance of the afternoon making their fruitless search, less for the outlaws than for a trail horsemen would use passing northward.

They eventually found a good trail, wide enough in fact for light wagons. Carter went down it looking for Henry and Jess Evans, eventually found them by watching a band of frightened deer rush blindly across in front of him.

He turned east, heard men talking, dismounted and was waiting beside a mammoth old over-ripe red fir tree when they came into sight. They were surprised to see him. They had not even found a good trail let alone where shod horses had passed along.

On the way northward where Gil was waiting, his hobbled horse hungrily cropping grass in a small clearing, the four of them came together. Al Henley was unhappy. He said very little as they prepared to bed down. Only when Gil jerked his head in the direction of a nearby upthrust tree, covered up its sides and across the topout, did he say anything.

'Marshal, if we don't find them by to-morrow, I got to leave you. I got a ranch to run an' this time of year we're real busy.'

Gil disliked the idea of losing Henley but had to agree with his reasons for heading back. As they hunkered atop the hill waiting for darkness and facing south he told the rancher they probably should all go back, their chances of getting a sighting of those renegades seemed not to be getting better, they seemed to be getting worse.

From the hilltop they could see one hell of a distance, daylight or darkness, from that eminence a cooking fire would be noticeable. The running men had to rest their livestock and by now they'd need rest too, and most likely cook a meal.

Nine

A Far-Away Place

For a couple of hours it was not particularly uncomfortable on their topout, but after that with night fully down and cold pinpricks of light above, the chill crept in, and they'd had no sighting of a fire southward.

With this kind of a vigil hunger was a two-way street, but no one mentioned it until Gil was finally prepared to abandon the vigil, disappointed and cold.

Carter made a dry comment that was probably not intended to make Gil feel any better. He said, 'They made a cold camp. All of us done it one time or another when for whatever reason we didn't make a fire.'

As the others arose stiffly to slowly work the kinks out, Jess Evans leaned on a tree staring northward. When Al Henley turned to say something to the cowboy, he too stood stone still, but unlike the cowboy, Henley said, 'That's no cookin' fire, that's lamplight from a square window.'

They all looked. The light was very distant and very distinct. It did not waver like a cooking fire, it glowed steadily.

Al Henley spoke quietly. 'That's either a village or a ranch, my guess is a ranch.' He turned to Carter. 'That wide trail we come back up here on — there wasn't no wagon marks but it was wide enough.'

Jess Evans finally straightened up off his tree as he said, 'Marshal, my guess is that if those bastards come down this way, they darned well might know where that outfit is. Now, on their way back ridin' tired horses . . .'

Gil nodded and led the way back down off the topout to the place where they'd left their outfits and animals.

No one said a word as they brought the horses in and rigged them out. Tiredness appeared to have dropped from each of them, even Carter Alvarado.

Gil's one unsettling thought was that, if there was another cow outfit back up in there somewhere, or maybe more than one or two, they might not find the renegades after all; it was not required of them that they try to get fresh animals from the ranch they might have raided on their way south.

He did not mention this, but as they were picking their way in the direction of that distant light, which they could no longer see, Jess Evans mentioned the possibility. Carter Alvarado scoffed. 'Hell, friend, if there'd been more we'd have seen more lights.'

This did not have to be the case but by

now they were fully occupied picking their way in and out among huge trees in almost total darkness. But at least now, as had not been the case on the topout, they could untie jackets aft of their cantles, shrug into them to keep most of the chill out.

Most rangemen had an inherent sense of direction. They might deviate a hundred or so yards in one direction or another but could easily correct an error if they had a sighting, and on a dark night that was what the Winchester men had after a couple of hours in the saddle.

The light was in the same location only much more noticeable when they worked their way toward a break in the timber. It came and went as closely spaced big trees interfered with the view ahead, but it remained constant the closer they got to an area where the timber had been thinned out, leaving only stumps, another sign that people lived close by.

In this kind of country log structures were not just the least expensive building material, they were created out of a resource that was close at hand and seemingly limitless.

The meadow they rode into from the forest was one of those large areas where grasses flourished but timber did not because of subterranean water very close to the surface. In wintertime this place would be almost a marsh, in spring, summer and fall, it would produce grass when other areas turned dry and brown.

The buildings which were silhouetted by starlight and the moon, were clustered on slightly higher ground. The closer the riders from Winchester got the more it seemed that this was an old ranch, for while the rooflines were unfailingly without any sag, the logs were a uniform weathered shade of grey.

That light they had seen was still burning, which made the two stockmen, Henley and Jess Evans, shake their heads.

It had to be one hell of a good reason for ranch people to still be up and about this late at night.

Gil told the others to wait and scouted up the place. Two dogs began to furiously bark. Gil could see the yard well enough with its buildings but not the dogs. He halted, rested both hands on the saddlehorn and waited. When the man emerged he did not leave by way of the front door, he went out a back door and sidled along the west side of the building. When he was at the point where the west and south walls converged, he halted. Gil could not make him out very well but there was no way to mistake the glint of sky-light off steel.

He called ahead. 'I'm Marshal Stevens from Winchester. I got three riders with me. All right if we come into the yard?'

The answer came back with very little hesitation. 'Ride on in, hands in plain sight.'

Gil signalled for his companions to follow, and entered the yard. Now, there were two lights burning in the house and the dogs left off their furious barking to skulk around behind the riders, growling but keeping their distance.

Gil swung off in front of the low-roofed, massive log barn and looped his reins. The man shielded by the house called out again. 'Walk toward the house, no carbines and hands in plain sight.'

Carter finished tying his animal and turned, scowling as he muttered. 'What the hell's he so spooky about?'

The obvious answer, which no one offered, was that anyone living in as isolated a place as this was, probably was only still out there because he *was* spooky.

They approached the house and got a surprise. The man on the east side of the house with a rifle was not the only one, as they halted within sight of the long covered porch another man spoke less stridently from the west side of the porch.

'Which one of you is the lawman?'

Gil turned in the direction of this speaker, whom he could not see at all. 'I am. Gil Stevens, town marshal down at Winchester.'

'You're a long way from home, Mister Stevens. What do you want?'

'We got reason to believe three outlaws are

118

heading north to Montana. We been trying to overtake them.'

'Three,' the calm-voiced invisible man said. 'You sure it ain't four? Some time back four fellers comin' from up north raided our remuda and left worn out horses behind.'

'If it's the same bunch,' Gil replied. 'I got one locked up down in Winchester. Did you get a look at them?'

'Nope; they caught our loose stock on the range, roped four horses and we never saw hide nor hair of them. But we still got their worn-down horses.'

'Branded?'

'Montana brands . . . You fellers mind puttin' your handguns on the ground until we can talk a little more?'

Even testy Carter Alvarado complied with this request. The way the man they could not see had said it made it less objectionable than it otherwise might have been.

They put their guns down.

The invisible man they could not see spoke to the man they could see. 'Go over them, Moe.'

The rifleman emerged from shadows carrying his long-barrelled weapon in both hands. When he was closer Gil thought he could not be more than seventeen years old. But young or not, he was business like and thorough. When he finished his examination and stepped back he said, 'No hideouts, paw.'

The other man came into view, emerging from darkness like a wraith. He had a sixgun in each fist. One of which he shoved into his waistband as he said, 'We just don't take chances.'

Gil nodded. 'I don't blame you.'

'About them four renegades; you think they're comin' back up through here?'

'We know they're heading north and we know they need fresh animals.'

'Do they know you boys is after 'em?'

'They just about got to know that by now.'

'You got a badge, Mister Stevens?'

Gil palmed it. The older man looked at the younger one. 'We can take a chance, Moe. Go tell your maw we got company.'

As the youth went up across the porch the older man stood in thought. 'How far down-country you figure those fellers are, Marshal?'

Gil could only guess. 'Maybe a day's ride, most likely less.'

'You think they'll come back through here? That'd be pretty chancy, them havin' raided us once, wouldn't it?'

'Not if you got loose horses on the range an' they find them. They'd likely do what they did before, help themselves without you knowin' anythin' about it.'

The rancher was grey, lean, rawboned and seemingly pretty much imperturbable. 'Pick up your weapons. I apologise for that but like I said, we can't afford to take no chances.'

As the five of them moved toward the tied horses the stockman said, 'You know these fellers?'

Gil said their names. He also asked if the abandoned horses had brands. The rawboned, calm older man replied curtly. 'Montana marks, Marshal.' He then proved that, slow-talking and calm-acting, he was not a fool. 'They'll be heading back where they come from, you think?'

'Yes. The feller named Hauser owns a ranch up there.'

The rawboned man halted where the horses were tied and introduced himself. 'Calvin O'Brien.' He then showed them where to corral their animals and personally pitched feed to the horses. As he was hanging the pitch fork back upon two nails he said, 'You're ridin' horses that got the mark of the way-station in Anselmo.'

Gil explained about that. Calvin O'Brien nodded and having fitted the pieces together, and also having made a judgment of his nocturnal visitors, he led off in the direction of the lighted house. As they were nearing the porch he said, 'My oldest boy's got the fever. My wife's been settin' with him. He needs some watered whiskey to break the fever but we don't have any.'

Carter Alvarado turned back without a word, entered the barn to rummage in a saddle pocket for his pony of whiskey and hurried to reach the others as they were entering the house, which was too hot and too bright. He, like his companions, had to squint until their eyes became accustomed to the light.

The youth called Moe was standing beside a leather couch upon which a tall, rawboned older man was lying, sweat dripping from his face, with flushed cheeks and too-bright eyes.

The woman seated at bedside with a pan of water in her lap used a cold rag in an attempt to bring the fever down. She looked haggard. When the strangers came inside she looked at each of them in turn then said, 'I don't expect any of you'd know anything about the summer complaint?'

Carter approached the sofa, he and the feverish man exchanged a look before Alvarado brought forth the little bottle as he addressed the haggard, greying woman. 'All my life, ma'm, I seen it treated by increasin' the fever until it's burnt out.' He handed her the little bottle.

Her husband crowded past Carter to lean and raise the sweating man as he said, 'Not too much, Martha.'

Not a word was said until the ill man had swallowed three times and was eased back down. Within moments the perspiration came in rivulets. The woman disappeared in another room and returned with a pitcher of water and a glass which she handed to her younger son. 'As much as he wants. Set here, Moe.' She smiled at Carter as she said, 'You boys'll be hungry,' which was almost an under-statement. They followed her into a large, lighted kitchen. She pointed to chairs at a circular table and as they sat down she got busy preparing a meal. There were no waste motions. The men from Winchester watched her while in the parlour Calvin O'Brien and his youngest son helped the ill man drink water until he finally lay back with his eyes closed, chest rising and falling.

Calvin and Moe came into the kitchen as the strangers were eating. They filled two cups with coffee and stood watching as Moe's mother piled more food on the table and the men around it continued to eat. Calvin made a dry remark to Gil Stevens.

'Been a while since you fellers shoved your legs under a table.'

Gil nodded without slackening off trying to find the bottom of his plate.

The woman left them to return to the parlour, but she was not out there very long. When she returned she looked enquiringly at her husband. 'Is he passed out?'

Calvin O'Brien smiled down at the woman. 'I think that's what they call it, Martha, but bein' a devout Christian I can't say from experience.'

Carter Alvarado had no such inhibitions. Between mouthfuls he assured the woman that was exactly what had happened, and went on to say if her son hadn't eaten lately, when he came round in the morning he might wish the fever was back because he was going to have the granddaddy of all headaches.

Later, when Calvin O'Brien went out onto the porch with the men from Winchester, he was still bothered by the possibility of those outlaws raiding his remuda a second time. With enough chill to the late night to convince all of them that dawn was not far off, he told his youngest son to saddle a horse and find the loose stock, and drive it closer to the yard.

Jess Evans volunteered to go with Moe and when no one objected, followed the lanky younger man around behind the barn where corralled horses were dozing.

Gil was building a smoke when the rancher asked what crimes the outlaws had committed down south. Gil lighted up and told him about the rangeman named Cotton who had died as the result of being shot in the back by one of the outlaws.

O'Brien considered that in his deliberate way, then made a suggestion. 'Maybe if me'n you fellers set up an ambush where they fetch in the loose stock . . .'

Al Henley liked that. So did Carter Alvarado who, with a full stomach, was willing to forego sleep to get this mess over and done with.

Later, he would dread the saddlebacking that still had to be done.

O'Brien said he'd meet them down at the barn and went back into the house. When they saw him coming a little later he did not have a shellbelt and a sixgun, he had *two* holstered sixguns and a Winchester carbine over one shoulder.

Carter leaned to speak in a low voice to Gil Stevens. 'He sure as hell didn't learn to use two guns runnin' cattle back in here.'

Gil's response was a curt nod.

O'Brien had a large herd of horses, mostly saddle animals running anywhere from eight hundred pounds to eleven hundred. He also had harness animals. Of his cattle, the men from Winchester had not caught a sight and would not until long after sunrise, there were about six hundred mammy cows.

They were saddling in the barn when Calvin's wife appeared. She had every right to be anxious. She could not leave her ill son at the house but her other two men were likely to be endangered and she was worried about that too.

Calvin walked with her back toward the middle of the yard with an arm around her shoulders. Gil, Carter and Al Henley acted as though they had not seen that. Except for Al Henley they were not married; it was embarrassing to them to see a man demonstrate affection in public.

When the two-gun cowman returned he accepted the reins to his horse from Al, led the way out back where they all swung across leather and as he was preparing to lead off he said, 'Gents; there's no cover for a mile or so westerly. If there's trouble, remember that. They'll be able to see us.'

Gil and Carter exchanged a look. So far they had skirted close to trouble several times and right now, in the event those renegades arrived up here, they did not have to be warned.

Calvin shrugged into a rider's coat that reached to his knees. He tucked the front of it back on both sides and again Gil and Carter exchanged a look.

It was downright cold. It was also dark, the moon was gone, the sky was black as Toby's behind, and except for the cowman who knew his territory, they would have had trouble finding their behinds using both hands, let alone three raiders.

Calvin was half a mile from the house when he drew rein, fished forth a plug and cheeked a cud. He looked apologetically at his companions. 'My wife thinks I gave it up years back.' He spat, picked up his reins and rode onward.

This time neither Gil nor the saloonman looked at each other. Calvin O'Brien was finally becoming a believable individual who wore two guns.

They did not ride fast and stopped often to listen. For a long time they heard nothing. Eventually though O'Brien raised a hand and halted. There were running horses coming toward them from the northwest.

Calvin lowered his arm, twisted in the saddle to look at his companions before wordlessly turning back the way they had come but on an angling northeasterly course.

Trees appeared like stalwart ghosts in a radius of no more than a hundred feet. They were closer to the yard and they were also the only trees close by.

Calvin O'Brien rode in among them, sat a moment listening, nodded his head and passed into dark tree shadows before dismounting.

Ten

Blood!

The oncoming remuda slackened to a trot, finally down to a slogging walk, and eventually stopped to mill and look back, but there was no sign of the pair of riders who had spooked them.

Among the trees men watched as the horses began to fan out a little and drop their heads to graze.

There was no sign of Moe O'Brien or Jess Evans, which did not worry the secreted spectators. Carter Alvarado asked their host where the nearest other ranch was and got a high, wide gesture. 'Northwest about eleven miles, over astraddle the stage road goin' north from Anselmo.' O'Brien dropped his arm. 'Westerly there isn't nothing but open country for as far a man'd ride in several days, and northward there's a big outfit owned by Canadians, that's got eleven riders.' Calvin smiled at Carter. 'If they didn't want to risk a raid up there comin' south I doubt they'll want to risk it on the way back.'

Carter was satisfied. 'That leaves you.'

O'Brien nodded his head and squatted at the base of a large tree.

They all got as comfortable as was possible. The cold was not quite as bad among the trees but it was bad enough. Carter curled up like a puppy and slept, something Gil explained to O'Brien. 'He's by trade a saloonman. This sort of thing's hard on him.'

O'Brien considered the sleeping man. 'Whiskey's the devil's seed, gents,' he intoned, staring at Carter. 'It'll make men do what they'd never even think about if they didn't drink it.'

No one pursued this and O'Brien fell silent. For a while the only sound was of grazing horses, until an owl came swooping in low to find a perch, saw the men, the horses, and with frantic pumping fought desperately for altitude. Its wings, usually soundless, made the only noise and it did not last more than a few moments.

O'Brien asked about the raiders. Gil told him what he knew with Al Henley occasionally nodding his head in confirmation.

O'Brien sighed. Over the years he had lost livestock to raiders, usually horses. It was one of the prices he paid for being so isolated.

There was a hint of soggy-looking grey all along the eastern horizon before Carter awakened, spat lustily, reached under his coat and shirt to scratch, re-set his hat, looked wetly around. 'Nothin' yet?' he asked.

Al Henley shook his head and mightily yawned.

Carter sat straighter and swung his arms. 'Marshal,' he said in a dead-serious tone of voice, 'There's got to be an easier way to serve the Lord than ridin' with you.'

That even brought a chuckle from O'Brien, the only man among them who took religion seriously.

Al Henley picked a tick off his wrist and was carefully positioning it between both thumbnails when he said, 'Marshal, if they're comin' at all it better be soon, or sure as hell they passed by in the night or took some other trail.' As he was afterwards disposing of the squashed tick he raised his head, sat a moment like a statue, and spoke again, in a softer tone of voice. 'I don't hear nothin' but look out yonder.'

They looked. The remuda was motionless, every head up, little ears pointing southward.

No one spoke nor moved until the loose stock began to gingerly back and fill the way horses do who have either picked up a scent or a sound that they don't feel easy about.

Gil got to his feet, jack-knifed his knees a couple of times and moved to the edge of their spit of pines. The others continued to sit until Stevens said, 'Horses. Ridden horses. Mister O'Brien, would that be your son?'

Everyone was standing up when the rancher answered. 'No. No reason for him to be down south. That'll be your renegades, Marshal. I'll bet you new money on it.'

Gil tried to juggle the time since they'd last figured about where the outlaws were, and now. It was entirely possible O'Brien was right, but if he was the outlaws had stopped somewhere, and that was not only possible, it was very probable. If they had neither seen or heard anyone behind them they might have decided the pursuit had given up and gone back, in which case they would not have continued to push their saddle stock.

If it *was* the wanted men and they were coming toward the same place they'd success-fully stolen range horses before, it was very possible they intended to do the same thing again, in reverse order.

The loose stock was beginning to evince increased uneasiness. Because of this it was not possible to hear the oncoming riders.

Gil wished Jess Evans was with them among the trees. He turned without a word to go back where their mounts were tied. The others followed without a word. As they were tightening cinches Gil said, 'It'll be day-light directly an' that changes things. They can see us.'

O'Brien, who had been through this before a number of times, made a suggestion. 'We can stay hid in here, let 'em bust into the remuda to rope some horses, then bust out after them.'

Carter clearly favoured this suggestion; he stood motionless beside his horse awaiting the marshal's reaction. Gil dropped the stirrup leather and nodded. The three of them remained with the animals, reins in hand. Out yonder the loose stock was beginning to edge clear. Like all loose horses their continued freedom was not to be compromised easily. Several animals broke away, heads and tails high in a loose gallop. Ordinarily this would have been enough to start all the horses to run.

Al Henley raised an arm. Visibility was poor but it was at least better than it had been an hour or so earlier. There was a rider to the west, too distant to be more than a wraith to the watchers among the trees, but close enough to create confusion among the loose stock. Some seemed inclined to follow the galloping animals, but with that horseman out there to block a concentrated rush, they hesitated, tossed their heads, snorted a little, and fidgeted.

Each of the watchers excepting the saloonman had been here before; while one man caused the herd to mill and fidget, unable to decide what to do, other riders came in a run straight at them, ropes poised. By the time the loose stock had their attention attracted from this new source, it was too late for quite a number of them.

Al Henley stood watching with professional

interest. As the ropers got to within lariat-distance he addressed Marshal Stevens.

'They're a hell of a lot shy of bein' green-horns.'

With men swinging lass ropes among them the loose animals exploded in all directions. Behind or alongside them raced the ropers. O'Brien went closer to the other watchers. He had the most concern in what ensued.

Three running horses were roped with the first casts. That rider who had approached from the west had a harder time of it. He was as good a roper as his companions but in his area fleeing horses were farther apart and breaking over into a belly-down run. They were out-distancing him; a saddle animal carrying a forty pound saddle and a man weighing in the neighbourhood of one hundred and fifty or sixty pounds, was handicapped.

But this rider was equal. After four horses raced past him in a headlong run he turned directly into the path of the following horses, made one swing and took two dallies. As the horse he had roped came to the end of the lass rope he was nearly up-ended.

O'Brien said, 'Now!' and turned to spring astride. He did not look back but the men from Winchester were close behind.

For a few yards the outlaws were too occupied with the animals they had roped to see horsemen bearing down on them, but when they did one man cast loose his dallies, drew his handgun and fired. His companions immediately let their ropes go and went for their weapons.

O'Brien fired twice very fast. He had the reins between his teeth, a gun in each hand.

Al Henley and Carter Alvarado tried to angle wide then close up in front of one of the fleeing men. He was looking back, sitting twisted from the waist with a gun poised to fire.

Carter hauled to a setting-up halt, took deliberate aim and was squeezing the trigger when the fleeing man saw him, and ducked low over his horse's neck. Even so that bullet tore the man's hat from his head and sent it sailing like a wounded bird.

The outlaw did not straighten up although he shoved his gun hand upwards and backwards, squeezed off one round and gigged his horse to its top speed.

There were abandoned horses trotting head-high and to one side to prevent stepping on trailing lass ropes. O'Brien and Henley continued the chase. Carter swung in beside Gil Stevens and showed a bloody sleeve. Gil told him to head back for the ranch and although he was some distance behind the others, joined the pursuit.

When he looked back Carter was riding low over his mount's neck still coming.

The fleeing men were scattered which

made it difficult to overtake them. One rider, Calvin O'Brien, evidently mounted on a particular horse, was closing the distance on an angling course which took him across the front of Gil Stevens and Al Henley. They could not fire until O'Brien was far to their left closing on one of the fleeing men whose saddle animal was either tired or just not fast enough to stay ahead of O'Brien's mount. Gil saw the flash when the crouching outlaw twisted to fire.

O'Brien jerked straight up in the saddle, hung there endeavouring to fire his guns, slipped slightly to one side and went off the horse head first, struck the ground with his neck and shoulders, rolled and fetched up against a stand of wiry mesquite.

Gil hauled back and to the left. Al Henley and Carter Alvarado shot past him.

The outlaws were holding their own but without gaining until Henley and the saloonman slackened off. The odds were too great; each outlaw was firing at them and granting the hurricane deck of a running horse was the worst possible place for accurate shooting, if enough lead was thrown someone would be injured.

When they got back where Gil was down beside O'Brien Al Henley sighed as he slowly dismounted and stood at the head of his horse trailing one rein, gazing at the bloody man Gil was working over.

Al Henley could see enough not to be hopeful when he said, 'Gil . . . ?'

Stevens did not look up. 'It was a lucky shot. Go get a wagon, put straw in it.'

Henley nodded without moving. 'How bad is it?'

'Get the damned wagon, it's bad enough.'

As Henley turned to ride away Carter came over, got down with a slight limp and approached close enough to see O'Brien's bloody shirt front. He did not say a word but took the reins of the horses and led them away to be tethered. He limped back as Gil looked up and asked about Carter's arm. The sleeve was bloody from near the shoulder to the cuff. Carter replied gruffly. 'It'll be all right. He don't look too good.'

Gil made no reply as he leaned over O'Brien, this time to start cutting away the red-soggy shirt. Carter put into words what the marshal had been thinking. O'Brien's wife already had one ailing son, she did not need a wounded husband, especially one who seemed to be in as poor shape as Calvin looked to be in.

Carter got down gingerly. He had wrenched a knee during the chase, how, he never figured out, but he knew it was injured the moment he dismounted.

Nevertheless he knelt across from Marshal Stevens, gently wagged his head and fished forth a rumpled blue bandana to wipe oozing blood from a wound that appeared to have struck the unconscious man just below the shoulder in front and had made a hell of a jagged hole where the slug had emerged in back, after either nicking or passing through the shoulderblade.

There was nothing either of them could do for the actual injury, which might not prove fatal although it was going to put a crimp in O'Brien's physical activities for a long while, but the bleeding had to be stopped.

They tried several measures, all of which helped a little but none of which actually stopped the bleeding until Carter tore part of O'Brien's soggy shirt, looped it over the shoulder and around the man's body below the shoulder, and cinched it as tight as he could pull it.

The bleeding dwindled to a trickle. Carter and Gil exchanged a look over the inert stockman. Carter grinned. 'I got no idea why it worked,' he said. Gil's reaction was that it did not matter *why* it had worked only that it *had* worked. He speculated that a medical doctor would have an explanation, it had been his experience they always did have one even during times when he had thought they hadn't known what they were talking about.

O'Brien was white and as inert as a dead man, but his chest rose and fell.

They cut the sleeve off Carter's bloody arm and wound it tightly above the gash made across his biceps. That too stopped the bleeding, something they understood would happen. At least in this instance they knew what they were doing.

Carter's only lamentation was about leaving his pony of liquor back in the parlour.

Gil wiped his hands in the grass, rolled and lit a smoke and squinted in the direction of the escaped outlaws. 'It was close,' he said.

Carter was far from resigned. 'We'll get 'em.'

Gil looked wryly at his friend and agreed. 'Sure we will. You with a wounded wing, me settin' here while they're still going.'

O'Brien moaned, his eyelids flickered but when they remained open the eyes behind them were nearly black from expanded irises, and glassy. They did not focus on the surroundings or the pair of men leaning over him.

Gil smashed out his smoke. 'Maybe he busted something when he went off the horse.'

Carter would not speculate about that. He wished harder than ever he had his pony of whiskey.

O'Brien tried to raise an arm. Between pain from the effort and the tight bindings he could not do it. The arm fell back to his side. He was breathing through his mouth, big, deep sweeps of air. Carter thought the binding across his chest was probably limiting the amount his ribs and lungs could expand but he did not suggest easing up on the bindings.

It appeared to be the lesser of two evils; if the wrapping that had stopped the bleeding up above were slackened, the bleeding might start again. If it wasn't slackened O'Brien would have to suck air, but at least he could do this.

The sun was climbing toward its noon-day high point before they saw a wagon coming. At about the same time O'Brien's eyes seemed to be focusing and the dilated irises were diminished. He croaked one word. 'Water.'

They had none.

The wagon seemed to take forever to reach them. Gil and Carter stared. O'Brien's wife was driving the team. Henley sat beside her. When she came up she did not look at either of the men beside her husband but got down from the rig, walked over and knelt.

O'Brien surprised Gil and Carter. He looked up at her and said, 'Sure could use some water.'

She arose, went briskly to the wagon and returned with a burlap-covered canteen which she held for her husband to drink.

Water revived him, perhaps not as swiftly nor as thoroughly as whiskey would have done, but his gaze went to the men nearby.

'They . . . got . . . away?'

Gil was going to reply when the wounded man's wife beat him to it. 'Moe and that cowboy are after them. They heard the gunfire. They were northward somewhere.'

Gil and Carter exchanged a look of alarm. A rider that didn't shave yet and Jess Evans, probably a good hired hand but probably no better than the average cowboy with weapons, and if that wasn't bad enough, they would be out-numbered.

Without a word they lifted O'Brien, carried him to the wagon, got him over the tailgate atop straw, and climbed back to the ground as the woman stood, hands clasped, faintly frowning at them. This time Al Henley had the lines.

Gil tried to make it sound casual when he said, 'We'll go find them, ma'm. You'n Al get him home to bed.'

They got their rested animals, rode past the wagon, looked down in and O'Brien feebly smiled at them. The woman said nothing as they both nodded to her and rode northward.

Several hundred yards on their way Carter said, 'How are they goin' to get him from the wagon to the house and into a bed?'

Gil shrugged as he studied the northward countryside. 'Leave him in the wagon. It'd be better than trying to move him.'

The sun was slightly off centre, there was

enough heat to make them cognisant of it when before they hadn't been.

Gil looked at Alvarado. 'It'll hurt your arm if we lope.'

Carter shook his head. 'My leg, not my arm, it's doin' fine. I eased up on the binding a little back yonder. Didn't hardly leak at all.' Carter set the pace by boosting his horse into a long lope and because the marshal was on the wrong side to notice it, Carter rode with his painful knee hooked ahead of the stirrup where each time the horse came down there was very little jarring.

Eleven
Getting Closer

For half a mile the tracks were scattered, after that they converged making it easier for the pursuers to stay on the trail.

There were occasional stands of pines which the pursuers avoided. They did not expect to be drygulched but every town had headstones in its cemeteries of men who had been careless enough to make this mistake.

They crossed a creek which was still showing roiled mud on its surface. They drank there, watered the horses and splashed across heading almost due north.

They saw cattle, wild as deer, a few antelope who stood their ground watching as the horsemen passed, and once, when the sun was slanting away, the trail veered near a foothill stand of trees, then veered abruptly back across open country again.

The same encounter which had spooked the fleeing outlaws made a run at them before they saw where the trail abruptly turned away; a black bear in her prime with a pair of small cubs. She made her charge from among the trees with surprising speed, slobbering and growling as she came.

If Gil and Carter hadn't gotten clear in haste the horses they were straddling would have done it anyway.

For a mile after the encounter with the sow-bear both animals went along with their heads up watching.

Later, with the sun lowering even more, Gil remembered something Calvin O'Brien had mentioned about a big cow outfit being up here somewhere. Eleven riders, O'Brien had said. It had to be a very large outfit to have that many riders. Most cow outfits, even the ones that ran a thousand cows, usually hired no more than four riders and a rangeboss.

If Gil hadn't been tired and hungry he would have appreciated the beauty of the wild country they were passing over. It seemed to stretch from one far curving of the earth to the other.

The farther they rode the more stands of overripe big timber they saw, usually to the east and west. The territory they were riding over was between those darkly majestic places, grassland like a sea of green.

When they came to a cold-water creek of good width and evidently also of a good depth, they dismounted to tank the horses again, and when their shadows fell across the water, trout exploded in all directions; the creek was apparently a spawning ground.

Carter waded in, sore leg notwithstanding,

corralled four large trout in a reedy place and flung them onto the bank.

As he came out of the water he grinned at the marshal. 'They're goin' to bed down somewhere up ahead.' He limped around gathering dry twigs.

Gil shook his head, hobbled the horses, removed the outfits and helped Carter make green-willow forms to fry the fish in.

As they were eating the sun balanced briefly on some distant rims and Carter said, 'Salt. Nothin' makes trout taste better'n salt.'

Gil ate two large fish, washed and drank at the creek, wished he could simply lie down in the grass and sleep for a week, went back to the fire and watched Carter gingerly testing his sore knee. Carter looked up. 'I never knew that. Ice cold water stops the pain in a sprung knee.'

Gil squatted. 'You lost ten pounds since we left town, Carter. Maybe we'd ought to do this more often.'

Carter was wiping his mouth with the only cuff still attached to his shirt when he replied. 'Y'know, we been friends a long time. Always got along good, never had no arguments — but I'm goin' to tell you for a fact, I'm never goin' horsebackin' with you again no matter what. Not even if someone like John Wilkes Booth comes running through the country with a big price on his damned head. Never!'

Gil built a smoke while replying. 'Carter, you need to get out of the saloon oftener.' He lit up and trickled smoke gazing at Alvarado. 'You need a shave.'

'*I* need a shave! Too bad we don't have a mirror. An' somethin' else; you know where we are?'

'No.'

'Well, you better hope when we catch those bastards in country like this where there's no town in any direction, because you're the town marshal of Winchester, Wyoming, an' unless I'm wrong as hell, we're either over the line into Montana by now or awful close to it — where you got no authority at all.'

Gil pitched his smoke into the creek and smiled. 'Carter, a town marshal's got authority only within the limits of his town. I had no authority since we rode past the hotel back in Winchester, but we got a trail with at least one killer at the end of it an' a couple other fellers darned near as bad. You rested enough? Because if you are let's get to moving . . . I'd sure like to know where O'Brien's son and Jess are.'

As they were saddling up Alvarado said, 'My guess is that by now they've given up and gone back.'

Gil did not know about Moe O'Brien, but he was a good judge of men and Jess Evans had not struck him as someone who would ever turn back.

He was right. But there was something else: A good judge of men does not necessarily include surmising what a good man will do under a lot of different circumstances, and because of that the marshal and his companion rode into an ambush in the only place trees came down far enough into the grassland for ambushers to set up once they saw pursuers, or at least some two men who sure as hell were tracking as they rode.

Gil's horse threw up its head. The marshal did not notice, he was squinting far ahead where a little blaze of light came and went intermittently.

Not until someone spoke as they were passing the trees did either the marshal or the saloonman straighten in their saddles. Carter had seen that fitful small fire too and was watching it. When that voice came out to him from the trees he yanked back to a startled dead stop.

The invisible man let a moment pass, then swore as he came out of the darkness. 'You should sing or whistle,' he told Gil and Carter.

It was the cowboy, Jess Evans. Behind him was Calvin O'Brien's son. Both were holding sixguns.

Gil masked his surprise — and embarrassment at being caught like a school boy — by asking if Jess and Moe had seen that distant fire.

They had. Jess was leathering his sidearm when he replied. 'That's them. We was sort of scoutin' up around to the north in case one of 'em slid past you fellers. They went past us like they'd been shot out of a gun on dog-tired horses. It was still daylight so we stayed in among these trees waiting for dark to go after them.

'That's as far as they went, up yonder where you see that supper fire. We was fixin' to stalk 'em in the dark when our horses picked up a scent back a ways. It was you fellers.'

Gil and Carter dismounted. The distance to that small fire was no more than a couple of miles and the night was not advanced. They led their animals into the trees, made them fast and hunkered in the tree-gloom. Gil did not tell them about the fight and the shooting of Moe's father, but he told them about the skirmish and the escape of the outlaws, something they had already figured out for themselves.

Jess asked where Al Henley was, which made it necessary, finally, to explain about Calvin O'Brien's wounding. Moe did not say a word, he stood up and walked back where the horses were, cinched up, swung aboard and without so much as looking back rode out of the trees for home.

The older men watched. Eventually the cowboy said, 'Can't blame him, they're a tight family, got to be in country like this where all you got to depend on is your own.'

Gil rolled and lit a smoke. Carter carved a sliver off his cut plug and cheeked it. There was a hint of cold in the night. That little distant fire was more noticeable as the darkness increased. Eventually the cowboy said, 'If we go slow we'd ought to get up pretty close in the dark.' Which is what they did after riding out of the timber on a northward course.

The little fire was a beacon. It was also a source of uneasiness for Gil Stevens. Those men had been almost caught stealing horses; they'd had to run for it. If Gil had been in their boots the last thing he would have done was stop. The second to last thing he would have done, if he did stop, was build a darned fire on a dark night with the possibility that he was being pursued.

Carter abruptly said, 'Y'know, Gil. If that's them, they aren't real smart having that fire on a dark night.'

Before the marshal could reply Jess Evans dryly commented. 'Well now, Mister Alvarado, there's another reason to make that fire. Put some sticks together, light them, then move off a ways, set down an' wait. If the fire burns out an' no one comes sneakin' up on it in the dark, why then there's more'n likely no close pursuit. If there is close pursuit an' they sneak up on that fire, those fellers hidin' back a ways could see that, couldn't they?'

Carter did not respond but this was exactly what had made Gil Stevens uneasy.

They rode quietly. After a mile or so they stopped conversing, which left only the soft sound of leather rubbing over leather and the almost indistinguishable sound of shod hooves in new grass.

When Gil could see the fire well enough he stopped. The three of them looked for outlines or movement and saw nothing of either. Carter half whispered. 'Mister Evans, you was right. It is an ambush.'

They dismounted and for lack of anything to tie to, hobbled their horses before starting forward on foot with a fair distance between them.

It required half an hour to get close enough for them to kneel in the grass. There was no one at the fire, no mounded horse equipment and no horses.

Without a word they turned back.

As they were removing hobbles Jess made another dry remark. 'Ain't no timber close, gents. There's some scattered brush an' not enough tall grass, so I'd guess they got to be lyin' out there in the brush somewhere. Thing is, a man lyin' flat on a dark night — you got to stumble over him before you know where he's at. But horses, bein' bigger and standin' up, they can be skylined even on a dark night, an' since we got four, five hours before dawn, maybe we could find their horses and set 'em afoot.'

Carter turned slowly from his horse to eye the cowboy. Gil did the same but neither of them said anything although their private thoughts were very similar. Range riders usually knew a little about cows, not anything about horses, and precious little else, but here was a feller right at home in a bad situation which he had taken to like a duck to water.

As they were riding again Jess gestured in the direction they had seen underbrush. 'Maybe if we scouted far out an' around, then set down an' waited . . .'

They let him pick the course and followed. He went so far out and around that when he finally stopped the little fire seemed farther south than it actually was. No one had fed more twigs into it so it was dying.

They dismounted, took the pulse of the chilly night, hunted for concealment for their animals then went back on foot. When they were within gun-range of the dying fire they stopped to hunker down trying to skyline for two-legged or four-legged silhouettes. When they saw nothing they crept a little closer. This time Jess left them to scout in an easterly direction. As soon as he was gone Carter Alvarado sprayed amber and shook his head. 'I think old Rufus hired himself some kind of cowboy who hasn't always been one.'

Gil nodded. 'He's handy, for a fact.'

Carter softly snorted. 'Handy! Partner, no one uses darkness like this lad unless he's done it before.'

Gil let the subject die. There could be any number of perfectly rational explanations why the cowboy was so good at what they were doing; none of them had to be that he knew something about being pursued in darkness.

Jess returned from the opposite side, from the west. They saw his silhouette before they heard him. He sat down and gestured. 'They ain't greenhorns. I think they're west of us in the underbrush. I'm pretty sure I heard a man clear his pipes.'

Carter asked if the cowboy had found the horses. Jess nodded and pointed westerly in the direction of some trees. 'Tied in there.'

'Someone with 'em?' Carter asked.

The cowboy shook his head. 'I don't think so, leastways I couldn't find no one.' He paused then showed his teeth in a rueful smile. 'An old man told me one time it's less what a man does that'll fix his wagon, than it is the mistakes he makes. Me, I'd have set right there on the ground beside my horse.' As Jess Evans arose and dusted his seat he made one more remark. 'The best of 'em gets careless, don't they?'

As Gil stood up he said, 'Not careless, Jess, stupid. Lead the way.'

It was quite a hike. Before they completed

it Carter's knee was troubling him again. Maybe ice water helped sprained tendons or whatever his trouble was, but it clearly was not a cure.

When they had the horses in sight Carter found a punky old deadfall pine and eased down on it. It did not require all three of them to cut the cinches on those worn-down, indifferent animals.

When Jess and Gil came back, one horse shook or shivered and his saddle fell off. That spooked the other horses. The moment they shied their saddles also came off.

Jess sat down with his back to Carter's deadfall, got comfortable and waited until the marshal also got comfortable before he said, 'You got a watch, Marshal?'

'No. If you're wonderin' how long before dawn I'd say maybe an hour, hour an' a half.'

Jess tipped down his hat. 'We got time for a little nap. If I was in their boots I'd come back for the horses just shy of sunrise, with enough visibility to look back an' see no one coming.'

Gil and Carter exchanged another of those enquiring looks as Jess Evans settled in for his nap. Neither of his companions napped although they were both dog-tired and Carter at least, had a throbbing knee.

They did not talk much either, for reasons that had less to do with being heard in the still night, than with their individual speculations about the mildly snoring man with his back to the old tree and his hat tipped down.

The cold increased steadily, as it always did just before dawn. Marshal Stevens went back over all they had gone through the past few days and shortly before Carter nudged the cowboy awake he thought about something Carter had said about this pursuit. Actually, he had not been in his own bailiwick since they'd left Winchester, and for all he knew right now they could be over the line into Montana where he would not even have the excuse of being in his own territory.

His conclusion was a basic one. He and his companions had come too far, had gone through too much to be overly concerned about legal niceties. Besides, after leaving that village back yonder where they'd dragooned the corralyard horses, they had not seen a single town or village, all they'd seen was a band of sheep and a fair-sized ranch. If there was more to this big-sky territory, it had to be some distance from where they were now scanning as much of the eastern horizon as they could see.

Gil arose. His companions did the same. Carter winced but ignored the pain. In his opinion they were closer to resolving what this was all about than they had been before; he could stand some discomfort just to get things settled so he could get back to his saloon, but he re-affirmed to himself what he had told Marshal Stevens. If the slayer of President Lincoln passed through he would not leave his saloon to join the pursuit. He also added something to that now. He was not going to get astraddle another confounded horse as long as he lived, or, until there was positively no other way under the sun to get somewhere.

They pulled back deeper among the trees where darkness lingered and would not entirely depart even after sunrise. They left tracks an Indian might have found but only if he was really looking for tracks. Pine and fir needles yielded underfoot but slowly recovered from being pressed down. It was unlikely that when the outlaws came for their horses they would be looking for sign back where they had hidden their animals, especially if they came in poor pre-dawn light after spending an uncomfortable night in the underbrush.

Jess Evans quietly said, 'They're goin' to see those saddles on the ground.'

There was no denying that. Jess lifted out his sixgun and let it hang at his side. Carter did the same, but not until he thought he heard someone clear his gullet and expectorate, a sound peculiar only to critters with two legs.

Gil said for each of them to pick a good tree and get behind it, which was done, but the wait was much longer than it should have been, or maybe it just seemed that long.

A man's raspy voice reached the hidden watchers. 'We got to change horses. Maybe they're not back yonder but you can bet your boots they will be. First chance we get —.'

Another voice interrupted. 'If we could rest 'em these horses might get us through.'

The raspy-voiced individual was evidently quick-tempered. 'Gawddammit, Blizzard, we can't take the chance. We got to have fresh, fast animals under us, an' right soon. No tellin' who's back there or how hard they're givin' chase.'

For a long moment there was no more conversation. Not until a man's voice sounded shrill as he said, 'What in the hell — *the saddles is on the ground!*'

Twelve
Worn Out Men and Horses

They could not see the outlaws. They knew about where they were from the voices but that was not enough. For a long moment there was no more talk and no movement. Eventually the man with the raspy voice spoke again, very quietly.

'Back out of here.'

Gil squinted to catch movement with his gun-hand rising. He saw one silhouette sidling toward a big tree but the other two were either not moving or had already got to a protecting place.

A familiar voice spoke in a normal tone of voice. 'Just stand where you are. Mister, I said *stand still!*' There was a pause during which both Gil and Carter tried to find the owner of that quiet voice. It belonged to the cowboy.

Evans spoke again, still without raising his voice. 'You're out-numbered and out-gunned. Move away from them trees and toss your guns away . . . You boys deaf? You don't have no more chance than a snowball in hell. *Move clear and shed the guns.* Mister, you're goin' to get yourself killed. *Do it!*'

Gil and Carter were scarcely breathing. It seemed that the silhouette Gil had seen, and which had stopped stone-still, was debating with himself. Gil cocked his handgun. The noise not only came from the opposite direction, it sounded unusually loud in the cold pre-dawn morning.

Carter did the same. He was more southward.

The shadowy silhouette swore under his breath and dropped a handgun.

Jess responded to that. 'Good. Now you two fellers behind the trees, an' remember, I'm behind you.'

The remaining outlaws shuffled forward and tossed down their sixguns. Jess raised his voice slightly in the direction of the marshal and the saloonman. 'Just watch close, I'm goin' over them for hideouts.'

Gil was impressed about the cowboy's behaviour. When he moved into sight from behind where the outlaws had been, he had his sixgun hanging at his side, and leathered it as he came up behind the first captive, roughly searched him and moved to the next one. This time he found a derringer in a boot and a knife, both of which he tossed away.

As he approached the third outlaw he said, 'What's your name?'

The outlaw looked bleakly at Jess Evans and did not say a word. Jess went over him for hideouts, found none and tapped the larger and older man on the shoulder. When he turned he moved directly into the path of a rock-hard fist. He did not fall but he was staggered.

'One more time, mister: What's your name?'

Again the outlaw glowered and hesitated. Jess lifted his sixgun and slowly cocked it. 'Only thing that's goin' to hear the shot, mister, is birds and maybe a critter or two.' He aimed the weapon at the outlaw's soft parts. 'Name?'

'Frank Hauser.'

Gil and Carter walked forward. The outlaws regarded them briefly before peering farther back as though expecting more men to appear. When none did one of the outlaws swore.

The captives were told to sit on the ground, which they did. Gil considered the hard-faced older man with the wound for a mouth. 'Frank Hauser. I got a prisoner in the jailhouse back at Winchester who told me about you.'

Hauser glowered but said nothing. He was probably not as old as he looked but years out of doors had lined and scarred him.

The man Gil was particularly interested in was large, not quite as large as the marshal, but thick and powerfully put together. He had close-set sunken eyes and a bloodless slit of a mouth. Gil said, 'Blizzard Blissel,' and saw the snake-eyed man's gaze widen. 'You were a troublesome kid an' evidently went on to become the same kind of a man.'

The third outlaw was nondescript. He had sharp, weasel-like features and pale eyes. He waited for Gil to get round to him watching everything.

Stevens sighed in the direction of the sharp-featured man. 'You got a name?'

The weasel-faced man did not hesitate. 'Sam Marly.'

Gil moved closer and looked down. 'That's not what Joe Lincoln said.'

The seated man's eyes shifted then returned. 'Eli McGovern, an' that's a fact. Ask Frank or Blizzard.'

Carter sought a place to sit. Jess was leaning beside a big tree. The tethered horses were fretting, they were hungry and thirsty. They looked as tucked up as gutted snow birds.

Gil squatted facing the captives. Carter was back a short distance. Jess said he'd fetch the horses and walked away. The malevolent-looking man called Blizzard made a darting circuit of his lips with a wet tongue. He did not like what he saw. The two older men who had caught them were stone-faced, cold-eyed individuals. The cowboy who had caught them from behind had departed; probably because he had no stomach for killings. Blizzard's tongue made another darting movement. Without waiting for whatever was to come next he said, 'It was Joe Lincoln shot that farmer's hired hand, it wasn't none of us.'

Eli McGovern chimed in. 'That's the truth.'

Frank Hauser was made of tougher material. He glowered at Gil. 'Who the hell are you?'

'Marshal Stevens from back down at Winchester where you beat hell out of an old man and raided some ranches.'

Hauser seemed to be turning that over in his mind. Not until he had arrived at some kind of conclusion did he speak again. 'Where's your badge?'

Gil palmed it then returned it to his pocket, and Hauser made a death's-head smile. 'You know where you are, Marshal?'

Carter, who had taken a strong dislike to the chief raider, growled at the man. 'Yeah; we're settin' in some trees tryin' to make up our minds whether to hang you sons of bitches or shoot you.'

That remark, plus Carter's villainous look, beard-stubbled, black-eyed and fierce expression acted like a physic on the weasel-faced man, Eli McGovern.

'It wasn't none of my doing. I just held the horses.'

Blizzard Blissel and Frank Hauser turned

slowly to stare at the nondescript man without either of them saying a word.

Carter did, though, looking contemptuously at Eli McGovern. 'You aren't worth the cost of a bullet or a rope, but suppose we give you *ley fuga;* you know what that means?'

McGovern shook his head.

'It's a game Mexicans play. They set a man loose, tell him to run an' shoot him in the back as he runs.'

Hauser put a cold stare on Carter. 'You don't scare nobody,' he growled, and Carter straightened up, moved forward with a gun in his hand. He stopped ten feet from Hauser. As they glared at one another Jess Evans arrived with the horses, astride one and leading the others.

Gil was going to speak again when Eli McGovern, convinced the limping man with the bloody arm bandage was going to shoot, spoke so fast he ran the words together.

'You can have the money back. None of this was my idea.'

This time, because Hauser was already defiant, when he looked at the nondescript outlaw he swore fiercely at him.

'You no-good son of a bitch. I'm going to break your damned neck.'

Carter took two steps forward and swung the sixgun. It caught Frank Hauser on the side of the face and blood spurted as Hauser went over backwards.

Gil moved between them. 'That's enough, Carter.'

Hauser, dazed by the blow, got back up into a sitting position with effort, fished forth a filthy bandana and held it to his face. If a look could have killed Carter would have dropped dead where he stood.

Jess went over to the grounded saddles and went to work plaiting cinch cords together. He did a passable job, and provided the horses did not buck or jump, the cinches would hold.

Gil helped him saddle the animals then ordered the prisoners to get astraddle. Jess removed the bridles, put lass ropes around the necks of each horse while Gil went among the prisoners removing their spurs.

The sun was up and climbing when the disreputable cavalcade turned southward keeping to cover as long as it was possible to do so, then rode out over open country.

Hauser's torn cheek bled and swelled. He ignored everyone except Carter Alvarado, who was again riding with his injured leg slung forward of the stirrup leather.

They did not halt until they were crossing through a gunsight pass where a creek ran. After watering the horses, Jess took Hauser's wet bandana to the creek, rinsed it in cold water and wordlessly handed it back to the injured outlaw.

Not a word was said as they resumed the

southward ride. When they were back down where the fight had taken place during which Calvin O'Brien had been shot, Carter growled at McGovern.

'If that rancher is dead when we get to his place . . .'

Gil waited for the weasel-faced man's reply. He had not encouraged Carter but he was content to allow him to show his temper; every chain has a weak link, Eli McGovern had turned out to be the weak link in this instance.

The other weak link was in the jailhouse down at Winchester.

This time, however, McGovern did not say a word. He may have been afraid to after the threat Hauser had made on his life.

Heat came into the day, the horses were thirsty again. Gil had heat on his back and would have drowsed along except that Jess called his attention to a pair of riders coming toward them in a lope.

Gil recognised Al Henley and assumed the other horseman was Moe O'Brien. He was correct. Where the two riders reached the marshal's party they stopped and gazed at the prisoners without saying a word. Gil got a sinking feeling behind his belt. He asked Moe how his father was, and dreaded hearing the answer. Moe was armed with a beltgun and a booted Winchester.

Moe did not reply, Al Henley did. 'We got

him comfortable. He lost a sight of blood an' is weaker'n a kitten but his missus is a good nurse.'

Moe had been studying the three prisoners, his gaze lingered longest on the beefy, soiled looking outlaw called Blizzard.

Gil nudged his horse, nodded to Moe and led off. Henley and the white-faced youngster fell in at the rear, back where Carter was riding.

They had covered several more miles before the youngster asked Carter which one of them had shot his father. Carter said he did not know.

Gil did not know either. It was possible none of them had actually seen the shooting, except the man who had done it, and whichever outlaw he was, no one expected him to answer in the face of the youngster's murderous look.

They watered the horses at a warm-water creek where trout minnows fled in all directions at the sight of moving large shadows above.

Moe O'Brien left Henley back with Carter and rode up beside Marshal Stevens. 'It was that beefy one, wasn't it? I'm goin' to kill him.'

Gil yawned before replying. 'I got no idea who it was, but your paw ought to.'

'He didn't see the feller's face, they was runnin' hard an' the feller dropped down the near side of his horse.' Moe paused then also said, 'It was a feller on a bay horse.'

Gil nodded. There were now nine men riding horses and five of them were straddling bay horses. Bay was the commonest of all colours in horses.

'What matters,' he told the youth, 'is that your paw is recovering. Be thankful for that and let the rest of it go. We've got them; they'll end up down in Winchester bein' tried for crimes committed down there.'

Moe was unrelenting but he slouched along beside Marshal Stevens all the way back to the ranch yard and there, with his mother standing on the porch watching, Moe helped unsaddle the horses. He and Al Henley pitched feed into their corral and joined the others out front of the barn.

Moe returned to the house with his booted Winchester carelessly carried over one shoulder. He and his mother briefly conversed before the youth went inside leaving his mother to call to the men from Winchester to make their prisoners fast inside the barn then come up to eat.

Al Henley produced chain enough to secure the outlaws to upright logs in the barn. When they were finished with that Frank Hauser addressed Marshal Stevens.

'I got friends up north,' he said, as defiant as ever. 'Even if you get us down to Winchester you'll play hell bringin' us to trial.

You was over the line in Montana where you caught us.'

Gil, Carter and Jess stood gazing at the chained man on the ground. Al Henley spoke. 'Mister, when you robbed me'n my wife and threatened to burn her, you made a real good enemy. I know that north country pretty well, an' I'll swear in court you was still in Wyoming when you got caught. There's others'll swear the same way; that old man you fellers beat, and other folks you raided.'

Moe appeared in the front barn opening to tell them his mother had a meal ready. He was carrying a carbine. 'I'll set with these sons of bitches just in case.'

Gil eyed the lad, held out his hand for the Winchester, took it and held out his hand for the sixgun too. Moe stepped back and nearly collided with the cowboy. Jess shoved a stiff finger into the youth's back, lifted out his sixgun and shoved it down the front of his britches as he said, 'You won't need a gun. They're chained.' Jess paused looking at Frank Hauser. 'But if they get bothersome you can use an axe-handle on them.'

Moe glared as the men from Winchester walked on their way to the house.

The daylong heat was at its height. A dog sprawled on the porch raised his head, watched the men enter the house and went back to sleep.

O'Brien's wife led the way to the bedroom where her husband was lying with an open window to one side in the west wall. He looked pale and weak, which he was, but his eyes were clear enough as the men from Winchester filed in.

He asked the same question his son had asked: Who had shot him? They answered him the same way they had answered his son. Gil asked if he hadn't seen the outlaw. O'Brien spoke a little sluggishly.

'No, not much to see, he was down the side of his horse.'

His wife herded the men from Winchester out to the kitchen, which was too hot, but that went with wood-fired cook stoves. She had piled platters of food on the table.

Ordinarily they would have cleaned up at the wash stand on the back porch, but after what they had gone through washing first was a luxury they did not even think about.

O'Brien's wife considered them, particularly Carter Alvarado with one sleeve left, the other one caked with dried blood around one arm. She had seen soiled, unshaven men before, but never ones that looked as exhausted as these men.

She left the room to confer with her husband and did not return until nearly all the food had disappeared. The guests were arising when she reached the kitchen doorway with two suggestions.

She and Moe would feed the prisoners, the men from Winchester could bed down at the bunkhouse.

Gil asked about her other son. She looked almost admiringly at Carter Alvarado when she replied. 'He's in his own room sleeping. That's about all he's done since the fever broke.' She smiled at Carter. 'Mister Henley told me your name. Mister Alvarado. I'm more obliged to you than I can say.'

Gil led the way back to the yard. Al Henley asked if the prisoners should be fed and Carter scowled at him but Gil agreed and Henley went back into the house.

They went out behind the barn where there was a large old stone trough full of spring water. Without much conversation they stripped to the waist, used their hats to trickle water over each other, stayed out there in full sunlight until they had dried off, then got dressed and entered the barn from out back.

One thing was clear; Blizzard Blissel and Frank Hauser had lit into Eli McGovern during the absence of their captors. McGovern refused even to look up as Gil spoke to the beefy man. 'Rufus is a tough old bird.'

Blizzard snarled about that. 'Cranky, demandin' old son of a bitch. Wonder to me someone didn't kill him long ago.'

'You tried,' the marshal said. 'By the way,

that feller who got the drop from behind you fellers back up yonder, works for Rufus.'

Blizzard's smokey gaze went to Jess and remained there. 'Not for long, cowboy. He's run off every hired man he's had since I was a kid.'

Jess shrugged. 'Maybe. I was lookin' for work when he hired me. I'll be lookin' for it if he fires me. But that might be a while. He took a hell of a larruping from you an' he's pretty old.'

Blizzard chose not to pursue this, his expression of hatred was fixed.

Al Henley appeared from the yard carrying three cooking pots. Behind was Moe O'Brien with plates, cups and eating utensils.

It must have taken a lot for his mother to get Moe to help Henley fetch food for the prisoners, men he would have shot without a second thought.

As Gil walked toward the sunbright yard he gave Moe a slight slap on the shoulder. Whether the youngster knew it or not, the slap was intended to convey approval.

The bunkhouse smelled musty and showed clear evidence that its only inhabitants in a while had been wood rats. It was too hot. Even after the two windows had been opened it still took the balance of the afternoon to cool off, but by that time snoring men, sprawled fully attired except for boots, hats and shellbelts, were dead to the world.

Thirteen

South from Anselmo

The sun was high before Moe came for the second time to summon the men from Winchester to eat, and even then they used up another quarter hour getting scrubbed and shaved, using someone's long abandoned razor that worried hair off more than it cut it off.

Moe helped his mother in the kitchen. She looked very tired and had every right to feel that way, she had spent the night in a chair at the bedside of her husband. When they asked how he was, she made a wan small smile. 'Every day he's still with me is to the good. I think he will be fine, but it's goin' to take a long time.'

Moe looked gravely at Marshal Stevens. 'You got a long way to go. You better watch Hauser.'

Carter was swabbing gravy with a bread crust when he said, 'That's one thing you can count on, son.'

They returned to the yard to bring in their rested horses to be saddled. The chained men had not been fed and Frank Hauser was profanely vocal about that. Gil asked Moe to fetch something for them to eat. The youth turned without a word heading for the house. As soon as he was gone Carter commented.

'That lad wants to kill you so bad he can taste it.'

When the food arrived the outlaws ate everything on their plates with Moe O'Brien leaning in the front barn opening watching them.

Jess and Al Henley rigged out the horses belonging to the outlaws then stood aside as Gil unchained them, ordered them to stand up, and allowed a moment for their cramped limbs to become workable. He then nodded toward the horses.

Blizzard and Eli McGovern mounted without delay but Frank Hauser paused to put a menacing look in the youth's direction. Moe glared back.

Gil gave Hauser a rap and the outlaw climbed astraddle with an effort. His face was a swollen mass of purple with dried blood on it. He looked bad but his expression of pure hatred made him look worse as they all walked their mounts out of the barn into the yard where Jess, Al Henley and Carter took the shanks to the unbridled horses, made a couple of dallies and nodded to Moe as they told him to thank his folks for their hospitality.

Moe did not move. He watched the riders

leave the yard in the direction of Anselmo. Once, when Carter looked back and saw that the lad had not moved, he rolled his eyes at Frank Hauser. 'You got a real bad enemy back there.'

Hauser sneered, 'He ain't dry behind the ears yet.'

Carter shrugged. Maybe not; someone did not have to be dry behind the ears to pull a trigger.

Eli McGovern asked for a chew which Carter reluctantly gave him.

It was a long ride to the village, the sun was high and hot, meadow larks sang in the grass as the riders passed, they saw a few cattle who fled, tails over their backs, and Eli McGovern tried to strike up an amiable conversation without any luck. Each rider was occupied with his own thoughts. Carter was ticking off the miles on his way home. Jess Evans admired the countryside, which was good livestock territory, apparently uninterested in all that was now behind him.

When they halted at a creek Carter ignored the others to bathe his swollen arm, wash off caked blood and work his fingers to see if the bleeding would start. When it didn't he left the sleeve bandage draped from a willow tree.

The arm had felt hot and awkward but was not as painful as Carter's knee with the pulled ligaments. But even that was bearable as long as he was finally heading home.

They had the village in sight by late afternoon, when all of them were hungry again. Without a word Jess loped ahead. Carter and Al Henley watched this. Gil said he thought Jess was going to see if there was a southbound coach at the corralyard and would try to delay it until they arrived, which was pure guesswork but Al and Carter said nothing. Carter, more than Al Henley, had come to have a lot of respect for the nondescript-looking cowboy. He had been with the cowboy throughout, Henley hadn't.

They were concentrating on the sighting of distant rooftops to the exclusion of everything else, otherwise they might have seen the loping horseman south of them about a mile.

When they arrived in Anselmo, rode into the corralyard and climbed down, the yard boss came out to stand looking at his ridden-down horses wearing a frown. He might have been sarcastic but as he watched the prisoners being helped down, saw their condition, particularly the man with the badly swollen face, and the sleeveless discoloured arm of the dark-haired and dark-eyed man, he said nothing.

Gil offered to pay for the horses and apologised for bringing them back in their condition. The yard boss forced himself to be civil, and shortly changed the subject. 'They'll be all right in a couple of days.

Those the fellers you was after?'

'Yeah.'

'That dark one don't look too good.'

Gil agreed. 'He don't for a fact. His trouble is that he's plain mean.'

Jess Evans walked into the yard. The yard boss saw him and grimaced. 'That feller behind you come awful close to threatenin' me if I didn't hold back the southbound coach.'

Gil smiled without looking around. 'He's anxious to get back. We all are. When'll the coach leave?'

The yard boss squinted in the direction of the sun. 'Hour. It would have left then whether your friend liked it or not.'

Gil nodded; it was a safe thing to say since there would now be no need to delay the departure, and saying it probably did something for the yard boss's self-image of himself as a tough individual.

People were watching from across the roadway when he and his companions herded the prisoners in the direction of the cafe. No one approached and no one said anything, but the cafeman did.

When they entered his place of business he was drying cups with a grey cloth behind the counter, and turned to make a slow assessment of the filthy, battered-looking men taking places at his counter. He said, 'You boys picked up some friends since that last time I seen you.'

Carter growled. 'Friends? We're goin' to hang them if we can. It don't matter what you got to eat, just bring it. And coffee.'

The cafeman departed smarting. Carter hadn't looked friendly at all. He had reason; now his knee was giving him hell again, but this time so was his behind.

None of the prisoners spoke, not even when the cafeman returned with heaped platters and asked if they wanted more coffee. Jess smiled at the cafeman. 'Sounds good.'

As they were eating people collected outside peering in through the only glass window. One of them was a large, coarse-featured individual with too-long hair and steely eyes. In a place no larger than Anselmo was they did not have a town marshal, they had a constable. He was the steely-eyed individual.

When Gil and the others left the cafe the constable was waiting. He seemed to be a direct individual because as they hesitated on their way to the corralyard he said, 'Which one of you Stevens?'

Gil nodded. 'I am.'

'Marshal down at Winchester?'

Gil dug out the badge, the steely-eyed man glanced at it and waited until Gil had returned it to a pocket before speaking again.

'I got the story day afore yestiddy from down the line. These the men you was after?'

Gil nodded again. Carter looked around for

something to sit on. There was nothing on his side of the road but across the way there was a bench beneath a sagging, weathered wooden overhang. He started limping over there. The constable turned and growled, evidently disliking the idea of one of these filthy apparitions getting behind him. 'You! Stay right here! You hear me? You with the swollen arm.'

Carter turned from the dirt just beyond the duckboards. Gil interceded; he saw the expression on his friend's face. 'Constable, he's got a hurt leg as well as a wounded arm. He needs to sit down.'

The steely-eyed man stepped far enough sideways so that he could see them all, including the man behind him. His right hand rested atop the saw-handle grip of his beltgun. 'You fellers got some explainin' to do. You took horses from the corralyard without sayin' why, an' you —'

'George!' a grizzled man wearing a storekeeper's apron exclaimed sharply from in front of a store.

The constable turned, recognised the storekeeper and his entire manner changed. 'For all we know the whole bunch is wanted somewhere, Mister Cogswell.'

The storekeeper's expression of annoyance did not leave. 'You saw his badge.' The storekeeper looked at Gil. 'Are you staying around?'

'No. We're going down to Winchester on the late-day stage. These three men with us are wanted down there for among other things, murder.'

The storekeeper shifted his gaze to the steely-eyed man. 'This is the second time,' he said. 'You been town constable seven days now. It's a good thing to be watchful and all, but George, you act like Anselmo's a big town an' you got to find outlaws everywhere.'

The steely-eyed man turned abruptly, crossed to the opposite side of the road and disappeared in a small building.

The storekeeper forced a smile. 'He's real protectful. I apologise. Have a good trip.' The storekeeper returned to his shop and Gil exchanged a look with Carter, who was still roiled. Jess Evans laughed softly. 'Badges got a way of bringin' out the bully in men.'

Across the road northward someone was turning the air blue because some pig-headed horse would not back straight to be harnessed, but swung his rump sideways. The profanity was followed by a sound of leather striking flesh.

Fred Hauser continued to gaze toward that store across the way where the steely-eyed man had disappeared. As he was being herded on a diagonal course to the yard he said, 'Them's the kind that makes folks hate lawmen.'

No one commented.

When they were in the yard Hauser wanted to wash his injured face. To relieve the aching, he said.

Gil nodded toward Carter. 'Take him with you. If the water's cold it'll maybe help your knee.'

Hauser hesitated about going with Alvarado but he went. When the hostlers who were hitching the horses saw them heading toward a stone trough, one of them addressed the other one under his breath. 'A man can tell from lookin' at them two they're outlaws. Especially that one with the limp.'

It evidently did not occur to either yardman that Gil would never have allowed two outlaws to go in search of a trough by themselves.

The yard boss came out of his cubbyhole office to collect for the ride down to Winchester. Gil paid him.

'There's a stop before you get down there.'

Gil knew this. All the men from Winchester knew it.

The yard boss eyed McGovern and Blissel. 'I got some chains you can use, Marshal, an' send 'em back on one of the northbounds.'

Gil thanked the yard boss and declined, but the yard boss looked long at Blizzard, who was a large, powerful-looking individual and repeated the offer adding a little to it. 'My brother's with the law in Texas. Twice he had 'em get away because they wasn't leg-ironed.'

One of the hostlers handed the lines to a small, bearded man who swarmed to the high seat and began evening his lines as he called downward. 'Climb in, gents.'

Carter and Frank Hauser were returning. Carter called to the driver. 'Hang on,' and limped as fast as he could. The driver waited until the last two of his passengers were inside then kicked off the binders and made a big circle of the yard so that his hitch was pointing directly at the roadway gate.

He was a seasoned whip. He nodded to the yard boss and yardman as he passed, cut a wide swathe to miss the gate posts and lined his hitch out southward.

People watched, even the steely-eyed man with a badge on his shirt. He stood with both thumbs hooked in his shellbelt. One of these days, not this time, but one of these days they'd ride into town and he'd nail them.

Day was ending, the sky was acquiring a burnished bronze look, daylight would linger for some time yet along with most of the daylong heat.

Carter rode twisted to one side. Across from him Blizzard Blissel curled his lip but kept silent. Jess Evans was paring fingernails with a clasp knife, unconcerned about the three outlaws across from him.

Al Henley fell asleep before they had gone two miles. When he fell against Gil the marshal gently eased him back upright, and he listed against Carter, who was not as considerate. He gave the rancher a sharp elbow.

The rig was old and rattled so loudly it was hard to hear anything else. It was also hung above old leather springs which did not respond to bumps except in one way, it made the body of the stage shudder and grind.

Al Henley was thinking of home when he said, 'My wife'd get down an' walk. These old coaches that sway and bump make her sea sick.'

No one addressed the three prisoners and they in turn made no attempt to strike up a conversation among themselves.

Blizzard was seated facing back the way the rig had come. He seemed interested in the countryside. Next to him was Eli Mc-Govern, Frank Hauser was beside the opposite window facing Jess Evans. Now and then, as he whittled his fingernails Jess would smile at the man with the swollen, discoloured face. One of those serene, taunting smiles.

Hauser stared out the far side window, his expression bitter and menacing. They had a good stretch of road ahead with excellent visibility. There were trees to the right a long way westward. On the east side of the road there was nothing until they were about four miles south of Anselmo, then there was a roadside jumble of large grey rocks, tumbled together out there by some upheaval maybe a million years before. They were a landmark, had been since bronco tribesmen had owned this country.

As the stage approached them the whip eased his horses down from a lope, as he always did when he reached this spot. It was his marker for hauling down and letting the horses walk for a mile or two.

Daylight was waning. There were still shadows, for example at that rock-field, there was a faintly discernible flow of shadows east of the big boulders.

Gil looked out and leaned back. Al Henley was awake looking about equal parts bored and tired. Jess had finished with his nails and had pocketed the knife as he sat staring steadily at Frank Hauser, clearly doing this to annoy the man with the swollen face.

McGovern tried again to get a conversation going, but this time whether he might or might not have succeeded, he was never to know.

They were abreast of the rock field, moving slowly past it when the gunshot sounded over the noise of the old coach. Gil and Jess reacted instantly by drawing weapons.

There was nothing to see but rocks. The whip reacted to a possible encounter with highwaymen by hollering up his hitch into a dead run. His passengers were thrown about. Frank Hauser, always alert, always the opportunist made a lunge for Jess Evans's handgun, got hold of it, was positioning himself to jerk hard when Gil leaned and pushed his Colt directly into Hauser's face.

The outlaw released his grip, Jess jerked his gun away. Gil settled back. Across from him Eli McGovern made a strange noise, barely audible but somewhere between a gasp and a choking sound.

He had thrown out his hand to brace against the tumult inside the coach, and was now holding it in front looking at it with round eyes. His fingers were covered with blood.

Gil yelled at Jess to get the whip's attention to stop the stage. Jess was successful, but only after he opened the door and climbed halfway up to the high seat and shoved his sixgun forward. The driver nodded and eased his horses down through their gaits until he could stop them.

They were about a mile southward of those grey boulders.

The whip went to the head of his horses, who were 'high' from their run. He stood up there looking down the near side as his passengers piled out. One of them, a cowboy, herded the weasel-faced outlaw and the man with the swollen cheek to one side as the other two men pulled and grunted until they had the other outlaw out and flat in the roadway.

Al Henley straightened up slowly. In a tight

voice he said, 'Dead.'

Gil knelt, peeled back the high side of Blizzard Blissel's shirt and stared. The bullet had probably been aimed at the head, which would have been visible beside the window, and while the bullet had missed the head, it had been damned good shooting; it had struck the big outlaw on the right side of the neck and had exited on the opposite side.

Blizzard was not bleeding but he had bled. There was blood over his clothing, inside the coach, and some of it had even splashed on Eli McGovern, who was ashen.

Fourteen
End of the Trail

Gil arose and joined Carter in peering back toward the field of big grey rocks. There was nothing to be seen back there, no sound either. Carter shook his head. 'Now what? We're afoot an' he's a-horseback.'

Gil nodded, dusk was settling, by the time they got back to that boulder field it would be dark. Too dark to read sign, even if they'd had the means to track the assassin.

Jess Evans was gazing at the dead outlaw when he spoke. 'Darn fool kid. Blizzard was goin' to get settled with when we got him back down yonder.'

Neither Gil nor Carter commented. Eli McGovern was having chills from the gory sight of the man who had been sitting beside him only a short while before.

Frank Hauser was strangely subdued. He may have figured the bullet had been meant for him. He would never know whether it had or not. None of them would.

The whip, still at the head of his hitch, broke the silence. His concern was for his coach and its horses. There was also a schedule but he had never tried very hard to maintain that. Moreover, although in twenty years of driving stages he'd encountered storms, wash-outs, grass fires and his share of highwaymen, he had never had anything like this happen before. The longer he stood up there with his leaders the more things settled into a decent perspective, so when Carter asked if any of his horses were rideable, the short bearded man answered with a bald lie because he did in fact have two combination horses in his hitch, he had no intention of having these men take them and go charging over the countryside in the damned dark leaving him stranded.

'Just harness horses,' he said to Carter, and added something else. 'You'd never find him in the dark anyway, an' I got a schedule to keep.'

Gil stood a long time in thought before nodding to Carter. Between them they picked up the dead man, grunted around to the rear boot and hoisted him into it. Afterwards they both had to dry their hands.

Gil jerked his head at Jess and Al Henley who were with the two remaining outlaws. 'Get in,' he said, sounding more disgusted than indignant.

Now there was more room inside, they braced for the shock of horses hitting their collars but the whip was considerate — for his horses not his passengers — and eased the hitch ahead without a jerk.

Frank Hauser looked worse in the ghostly light than he looked in daylight. He glared at Marshal Stevens. 'You goin' to let that pipsqueak get away with murder?'

Gil looked blandly at the outlaw. 'What pipsqueak?'

Hauser glared. 'You know damned well who done that.'

'Who?'

'That damned kid back yonder.'

Carter entered the discussion with a mild question. 'You saw him, did you?'

Hauser looked balefully at them, did not say a word but turned to look out the window into the settling darkness.

Gil gazed at Eli McGovern wondering what kind of a man rode with outlaws, robbed people, saw them get beaten, watched as a woman's feet were going to be put into a hot stove, and now, caught and surely going to prison, lost all his guts.

By the time they reached Appomattox there were only two or three lights the full length of Main Street and it was getting as cold as a witch's bosom.

When they wheeled up into the stage company's big palisaded yard the whip was ready to set the binders, fling the lines down and climb down to the ground like a spider going down a wall. He did not even look back but hurried toward the lighted office of the yard boss and was telling his story to a baggy-eyed

186

man who had been sleeping in a chair when he burst in, before his passengers were out of the coach.

Two sleepy yardmen came forward to change the hitch. One of them moved sluggishly around the coach, stopped stone still as he called to his companion. 'Art; there's a dead man in the boot.'

Jess walked back there leaving the marshal and his two companions to care for McGovern and Hauser. As the second yardman went behind the rig Jess said, 'He had an accident.'

One yardman looked at Jess. 'Some accident; shot through the neck.'

The yard boss along with the whip came out there, went directly where the yardman and Jess were standing, and as the yard boss looked at Blizzard, his hostlers shuffled ahead to complete the change of horses.

The yard boss already knew what had happened and he had recognised Marshal Stevens. He looked at his driver, shrugged, said nothing, walked back to his office and slammed the door.

Gil was not as hungry as he was thirsty for something to get his body warm, but the saloon was dark and locked tight. Frank Hauser growled about being cold and hungry. Gil smiled at him. 'We all are.'

What normally might have taken half an hour, getting a fresh hitch hooked to the coach, took only about half that time. When everything was ready they drove their prisoners inside, piled in after them and the whip made his wide turn to head out of the yard. He walked his fresh hitch the full length of town and a fair distance beyond before boosting the horses into an easy lope.

It got colder the longer they were on the road, the whip was huddled into an old moth-eaten buffalo robe coat that reached to his knees but the men inside the coach were not that fortunate.

The only one of them who seemed unaware of the cold was Eli McGovern; in the pale light he resembled a wax dummy.

Carter slept. With more room inside he could lean without bothering anyone. Jess, again directly opposite Frank Hauser, seemed tireless. He rolled and lit a smoke, smiled a little at the outlaw and when Hauser turned aside refusing to meet the cowboy's stare, Jess's smile broadened.

They made two stops at turn-outs before reaching Winchester. At each stop everyone piled out to stretch and swing their arms. At one of the stops Al Henley asked Frank Hauser where his money was, and got a snarl for an answer.

Carter, looking for such an excuse, limped over and poked Hauser with a stiff finger. 'The man wants his money.'

Gil saw serious trouble coming and called

to Carter. The whip had finished checking everything and was climbing to his high seat. They got back in, Hauser malevolently sulky and Eli McGovern still acting like a sleep-walker.

Between the last turn-out and Winchester, a fair distance, scarcely a word was said. Carter snored, Eli looked incapable of hearing or seeing, and Jess Evans musingly watched the night slide past.

Gil was back in familiar country. He rolled and lit a smoke. In his absence it was customary for the cafeman to feed prisoners so he did not worry about Joe Lincoln. He had ghostly rooftops in sight before he wondered about old Rufus. He did not think about the money the raiders had stolen until they were going down Main Street in a slow walk with trace chains rattling.

The Winchester corralyard, like most others in towns large enough to afford a bunkhouse for yardmen, corrals and a fair-sized front office, had someone awake all night. This night the hostler was a fiercely-mustachioed rawboned man with sandy hair and pale blue eyes. He stood at the head of the horses until the whip was on the ground, then barely nodded to the driver as he worked his way toward the coach unhooking single trees and snapping traces into place.

The whip told the yardman about Blizzard in the boot. The yardman nodded absently and returned to the leaders to lead the horses away to be unharnessed and turned out. The driver stared after him. He turned as Gil came up. 'I told him there was a dead man in the boot. Hell you'd have thought I said it looked like rain.'

Gil shrugged, got McGovern and Hauser lined out in the direction of the jailhouse and started walking. Al Henley, who had a horse down at the liverybarn, remained with the procession until everyone was inside, then he nodded to Gil and went for his animal. He still had a long ride before reaching home and probably would not make it until after daybreak.

Gil got a lamp lighted. In good light he gazed at Hauser and McGovern; they looked like something a dog might have dragged in. Gil told them to empty their pockets. Under the eyes of Gil, Carter Alvarado and the cowboy, it gradually became clear that a division of stolen money had been made. Jess turned toward the door as he said, 'I'll go get whatever the dead one has,' and departed.

Gil fired up the office stove, put the coffee pot atop it and gestured for Hauser and Mc-Govern to be seated while he unlocked the cell room door.

Jess Evans returned with a hatful of the dead man's personal belongings including a fair-sized roll of greenbacks. As he put the hat on the lawman's desk he glanced at Frank Hauser. 'Which of you shot that old cowboy in the back?'

Hauser did not hesitate when he replied. 'You got his hat on the table.'

Eli McGovern stared at Hauser. Jess saw that and re-phrased his question. 'I know better. You shot him didn't you?'

'That's a damned lie.'

'Eli told me you did.'

Hauser turned on his fellow outlaw. 'You snivelin' son of a bitch.'

McGovern was speechless. It had happened too fast. He was about to speak when Jess addressed Hauser again. 'Those folks at the ranch saw you step in front of the barn doorway and shoot.'

Hauser snarled at Jess. 'In the damned dark? They didn't see nothing. The house was too far for them to see me step into the doorway.'

Jess grinned slowly. When Gil returned from the cell room Jess nodded in Hauser's direction. 'He just said he shot that old cowboy called Cotton.'

Hauser exploded. 'I never said no such a thing! This idiot made that up!'

Jess continued to half-smile. 'You just told me the house was too far for the folks over there to see when you stepped into the doorway of the barn. That's where the killer was standing when he fired.'

Hauser came up off his bench snarling like a cornered animal. Gil told him to sit back down, which Hauser did not do. He turned his fury on Eli McGovern. 'You lousy bastard. You sniveling —'

'I didn't tell him you did it. He said that to trap you. But it's the gospel truth. When that feller run into the yard you stepped out there and shot him in the back.'

Hauser remained upright, stiff, with both fists clenched. Jess spoke quietly to the town marshal. 'You better not put 'em both in the same cell.'

After Gil took his prisoners down into the cell room, Jess sat down, built a smoke and was lighting it when the marshal returned, slammed his cell-room door, barred it from the office side, went to his desk and sat down, tossed his hat aside and ran a hand over his face. He was tired enough to sleep for a week.

The cowboy waited out a long silence between them then leaned to kill his smoke and arise as he said he'd better get back to the ranch; there'd be horses out there needing feed and chores to be done.

Gil leaned back regarding Evans. He wanted in the worst way to ask some personal questions but from the resolute look of the cowboy, he doubted that he'd get any enlightening answers, most likely no answers at all. He said, 'I'm obliged, Jess. Those folks they robbed will be too, and in case old Rufus gets too hard to live with, come on back to town, there'll be a place for you.'

The cowboy stood a moment in the doorway with cold dawn breaking, smiled at the town marshal and departed.

Gil went up to the corralyard on his way to the hotel where he lived. They had already stowed Blizzard in a storeroom with a soiled old canvas over him. Gil told the hostler he'd have the town carpenter, who was also the undertaker, get the body later in the day, and didn't miss Carter until someone called to him from the poor, grey light over in front of the saloon.

'You get 'em settled in?'

'Yeah. Hauser killed that old cowboy, shot him in the back.'

Carter was in his saloon doorway. 'That's no surprise. Too bad you only got Hauser to get hanged.'

'See you tomorrow afternoon. Hope your leg's better,' the marshal exclaimed.

Alvarado nodded. 'It's feelin' better already. So's my arm. Stand a round when you show up in the afternoon.' Carter started to enter his saloon, paused, then turned to call again. 'How about the cowboy?'

'He went out to the Irons place to look after things until old Rufus can get around.'

'Next time you see him tell him I got a job for him at the saloon. I been needin' an extra

193

hand for some time.'

Gil nodded and continued on up to the hotel where he barely got flat out before he fell asleep.

The following late afternoon they buried Blizzard Blissel. Carter and the town marshal were the only ones present except for the grave diggers.

It was early evening, after Gil Stevens had eaten a big meal at the cafe before going up to the saloon to collect that free drink, when he and Carter mentioned some loose ends, one of which was how Gil would get the money back to the folks who had been raided.

That posed no problem. Gil would ride out to the ranches in a day or two with the money. If it wasn't all there, he could do no more than divide it among the victims but he told Carter it was probably all intact since the fleeing outlaws hadn't had a chance to spend it.

Carter said his knee was much better, and, wearing a fresh shirt, there was no outward sign of his other injury. He too had slept the clock around. As he leaned on the bar looking at Marshal Stevens he asked about Jess Evans.

Gil told him of events at the jailhouse before Jess had departed. Carter digested all that before making a comment of his own.

'He's *coyote*, Gil. A man don't get that way

starin' at the rear end of cows.'

The marshal agreed. 'Yeah. I wanted to ask him a little about himself last night, but I didn't.'

Carter nodded understandingly. 'Next time he comes to town maybe we can talk to him.'

There was no 'next time'.

Rufus drove his old wagon back to his ranch two weeks later, not fully recovered but well enough to go from day to day by taking it easy.

Two weeks after that he drove the wagon into town for supplies. He looked good and if a man's recovery depended on how soon his disposition returned to normal, old Rufus was in good shape. He complained to Carter about the whiskey he was served. He complained about the weather; cattlemen liked rain every two or three weeks and with summer on the land they were very unlikely to get it.

He was feeling his first drink in some time when Gil Stevens walked in. Rufus eyed the large man. 'Jess told me the whole story. I was kind of hopin' that Blissel feller would come back with you'n Carter. I wanted to settle with him.' Both younger men exchanged a look and both smiled. Rufus had fully recovered; at least in the head and temper. The old man then said something that stopped both his listeners in mid-breath.

'Jess quit me couple days ago, said he'd

seen enough of this country, wanted to look on the other side of a few more mountains.'

Gil frowned. 'You ragged him into it like you did the others?'

Rufus turned on the large man, red in the face. 'I never ragged him. I been waitin' years for the right man to come along. Jess was him; good with animals, knew what to do without no telling. We got along pretty well. Wasn't no bigger surprise to me than it is to you. He just come in after chores day before yestiddy, said he wanted to draw his time, saddled up and rode out.'

'Did he say where he was going?' Gil asked.

Rufus shook his head. 'Didn't say much of anythin' except what I already told you — wanted to see the other side of the mountains. Well, don't stand there starin'. They do that. I don't know why unless it's an itchin' heel. One day they're working and the next day they draw their wages and ride off.'

Jess Evans was never seen in the Winchester country again. The few people who had known him speculated for a long time without ever coming up with anything verifiable.

The following winter, cabin-bound by snow two feet high and a raw wind, Carter and Marshal Stevens sat by the stove at the jailhouse sipping coffee as black as original sin, long after Frank Hauser and Eli McGovern had been tried and sentenced to hang, when the clerk from the general store brought over the marshal's mail, which included among other things, a wanted dodger from Idaho for a man who was wanted for murder.

The dodger gave only the minimum details. The fugitive whose likeness stared from the front of the poster, had killed a man who had robbed and strangled an old woman for her money. The killer had been chased down by the fugitive whose picture looked back at Carter and Gil Stevens, had been overtaken by him and despite the fact that the strangler had not been armed had shot him to death.

The face on the dodger was that of Jess Evans, but the name was different.

Gil took the dodger to the stove, shoved it in, both men watched it burn to a cinder, then went back to drinking their coffee without saying a word.

The employees of Thorndike Press hope you have enjoyed this Large Print book. All our Thorndike and Wheeler Large Print titles are designed for easy reading, and all our books are made to last. Other Thorndike Press Large Print books are available at your library, through selected bookstores, or directly from us.

For information about titles, please call:

(800) 223-1244

or visit our Web site at:

www.gale.com/thorndike
www.gale.com/wheeler

To share your comments, please write:

Publisher
Thorndike Press
295 Kennedy Memorial Drive
Waterville, ME   04901